HIS NEW PLAYTHING

EMILY TILTON

D1509744

Published by Stormy Night Publications and Design, LLC.
www.StormyNightPublications.com

Tilton, Emily
His New Plaything

Cover Design by Korey Mae Johnson
Images by Shutterstock/tazzilla and Shutterstock/voyata

CHAPTER 1

 sabella

Luxury sponsors never went for girls over thirty. That's what all the girls on the Selecta Arrangements forums said. I knew when my birthday came and I still hadn't found one that my chance at a real happy ending had flown away.

Thirty. I'm thirty, I kept telling myself, and I didn't really have a clue how I felt about it.

On the one hand, I couldn't help feeling a good deal of pride at having actually lived this long in the shitty world of the energy collapse and the corporate laws. I had fled a home that was more like a hell at age eighteen. I had found my way into various Selecta Corporation programs that kept me fed, housed, and clothed—surviving much more, if I said so myself, on my wits than my reasonably good-looking face and slim but still under-developed body.

I had made it to thirty with my sanity intact, in a world where young people seemed to get chewed up and spit out into the labor camps with frightening regularity.

On the other hand, I had nothing to show for it.

Three years as a data entry specialist at a Selecta subsidiary that made rechargeable batteries. The typing class in the Selecta-sponsored education facility had prepared me for that. Five years as a data entry specialist manager, making a little more, with the prospect of actually being admitted into an executive training program.

Except that the market for rechargeable batteries had evaporated when the rare earth minerals (not that I had any idea really what that meant) had stopped coming from the mines, as war overtook the countries producing them.

Two years, after that, waiting tables at a Selecta corporate retreat. Dead-end hardly begins to describe it. The only decent part laid in the way Selecta did fulfill their promise to pay their employees a living wage, no matter how lowly.

Then, at twenty-eight, a fellow waitress had told me about the Selecta Arrangements program. I knew it would involve rethinking the way I approached romantic relationships. I could see through all the marketing materials about *Love on your terms.*

Knowing I was already past the prime age for finding the wealthy sponsors, I had settled for moderate sponsors, and I had, to be fair, had two relationships with kind men that had let me enjoy some of their small slices of prosperity.

Nice meals, nice clothes. Things I couldn't have afforded on my waitress salary, even living in Selecta-subsidized housing. Nor had either of these guys been interested in what seemed to me the dark side of Selecta Arrangements: the disciplinary part.

Of course, I hadn't done anything sassy, either, or even been late to a date. So the matter of *consequences*—as the girls usually put it on the forums—had never come up with either guy.

Neither had marriage, though. Both arrangements had ended quietly, with the guy telling me he had found another young woman. They hadn't said that the girls they had found were younger than me, but I knew how it worked.

Thirty. I sighed, looking down at my handheld where I had the Selecta Arrangements app open. *Time to start looking in the bargain basement.*

My finger had started to hover over the *Economy* button in the search filter. If I tapped, I would see the many, many guys who weren't able, or in some cases willing, to put that much money into having male-led sex with the promising young women Selecta had curated for their enjoyment.

3

A lot of these guys, the forums told me, did want to get married. Once they had found a mate, after all, they wouldn't have to pay Selecta's membership dues anymore. I would never have a yacht, but at least I would have a decent guy who appreciated me. That had always seemed to me the true promise of Selecta Arrangements, along with the one-in-a-million shot at the trillionaire you hit it off with, so that he sweeps you off your feet with a proposal... and a yacht.

An alert popped up.

"An invitation from Selecta: based on your profile, Isabella, you may qualify for a new SA program! Tap here to learn more."

I was sitting in my dark living room with no prospect of going anywhere soon, about to take what seemed an irrevocable first step on a downward spiraling path. Given what everyone knew about Selecta, they had probably sent the alert for precisely that reason. Did their algorithm see that it was my thirtieth birthday, and that I hadn't even gotten a cake for myself, let alone anyone else providing it?

It hardly mattered. I tapped the alert.

Especially for our associate members thirty and older! Would you like to participate in exciting, cutting-edge research, with a guaranteed one-year luxury subsidy?

My jaw dropped. A button at the bottom seemed to draw my fingertip like a magnet.

Join the longevity study.

"Longevity?" I murmured. It could mean so many things.

I tapped the button. A screen full of text appeared. At the bottom, the *I agree* button was gray. I groaned.

I didn't read, I scrolled past all the text. I had already signed my life away to Selecta, hadn't I? I mean, I had agreed to accept a spanking from the guys I dated, if they thought I needed one.

Once I had scrolled through what was probably ten thousand densely-packed words, at least, the button turned blue. I tapped it.

Screening appointment scheduled for May 5 at 8am at your residence. Please pack a bag for a three-day trip and be ready to leave immediately if you are accepted into the intensive program.

My jaw dropped again. The next day. Tomorrow morning.

I instantly regretted not reading the contract to which I had just agreed, of course. I tried to go back and figure out where exactly I had said I would leave at the drop of a hat for parts unknown. I found the contract, but the wall of text defeated me the moment I started: *This agreement binds the parties undersigned to a covenant under statutes 37(a), 37(b), 76(f), 98(a)...*

Well, at least I knew Selecta ran everything, including the clothing store where I worked. If they were going to take me into some research project deep in their machinery, they would at least give my boss notice and make sure my credit rating didn't suffer.

Because they literally *owned* the credit bureaus, the forums had told me.

I sighed and stood up and headed for my tiny bedroom. I had no idea what I had gotten myself into, but with a year of luxury subsidy coming my way, I felt like I could sleep easy.

The buzzing alarm woke me at seven, which was half an hour earlier than I had it set. Ugh. Fucking Selecta. They controlled everything in the apartment, of course, and had clearly reset the alarm to make sure I would be ready for the weird appointment it took me ten seconds to remember—before I looked at the display on my bedside table and read *LONGEVITY PROGRAM SCREENING, 8AM.*

What the fuck had I done? As if to answer me, my hand-held buzzed on the nightstand. When I picked it up, I saw an alert that made my heart beat faster, but in a very, very good way.

DEPOSIT FROM SELECTA RESEARCH.

I tapped and my eyes went so wide I felt like a comic book character. *That* was what I had done. I sighed. My luxury sponsor was an arm of our corporate overlord, and I felt fine. If accepted, I would have to depart immediately, but surely, I would be coming back soon... should I think about applying for a bigger apartment, though?

And the point of this cutting-edge program must be to help me find a real luxury sponsor, right? I couldn't see any other reason, since one of the many things everyone knew about Selecta is that they liked taking wealthy people's money—what else could they intend for me but that I be a source of revenue?

My brain went over and over those questions in a frustrating, endless loop as I packed a backpack, showered, and looked at myself in the mirror. Knowing Selecta, and Selecta Arrangements, as I did, I had no doubt at all that my appearance would have an important role in whatever research they meant to make me a part of. I regarded myself naked in the full-length mirror with which SA so helpfully provided in each of their subsidized apartments —the better to ensure that "associate members" like me could make themselves as appealing as possible to the "full members" who took them on dates, gave them allowances… and, of course, paid a substantial fee to Selecta.

Thirty. I refused to fool myself. I could see small lines around my eyes. I had found a grey hair and plucked it three days ago. My tummy, once so easy to keep board-flat despite eating french fries on a weekly basis, protruded enough that I wore shapewear on dates these days.

My breasts, so little that I could count on two hands the times I had worn a bra in the last five years. Three of those times had been because my last sponsor had said a certain actress looked hot in a lingerie set in a movie we had watched—then bought me a similar set. He had fucked me enthusiastically in them the first time, then progressively less enthusiastically on subsequent dates. I had finally decided I just didn't have the cleavage to look at all like the actress—though her breasts weren't really *that* much bigger than mine—and that my sponsor must have come to the same conclusion. I had gone back to not wearing a bra, and his twice-weekly fucking—never terribly animated to begin with—had returned to normal.

Like my previous sponsor, he had clearly chosen me in part because of my elfin figure; some guys just liked that, the way some guys among the SA member crowd liked a little patch of hair above a girl's pussy, or even a fully developed, neatly trimmed bush. A few guys, according to the forums, even demanded that their SA girls let their pubic hair grow freely.

My sponsors had both proven more generic in their taste. Though I had let the brown curls between my thighs go for a couple weeks before this morning, I had just shaved them in the shower. SA's basic instructions, provided by the counselor who had admitted me to the program, included keeping your pussy bare unless a sponsor instructed you otherwise.

Looking down there now, in the mirror, sent a blush to my cheeks that I could see when I raised my eyes to regard my heart-shaped face, framed in light brown hair, currently pulled back into a ponytail. My conventional brown eyes looked back at me. I looked into them in search of the reason it still made my face hot to think about shaving my pussy.

Something about what it seemed to mean—about the control Selecta had taken over my body, and then handed over willy-nilly to the men who decided they might like to date me... no... might like to *fuck* me. Might like to enjoy the place I had been made to bare for their inspection and their pleasure.

I bit my lip and turned away from my reflection, to put on my everyday pink cotton panties, then my jeans and my t-shirt. I heard a buzz from my handheld.

SELECTA SCREENER HAS ENTERED YOUR BUILDING.

I looked at the time. *Shit.* I had lost five minutes to my reverie in front of the mirror.

I heard the doorbell. Finishing tugging my t-shirt over my chest as I went, I crossed the living room to the door. I took a deep breath, then opened it to reveal a middle-aged woman in scrubs. Everything about her said *nurse.* I had never loved going to the doctor. My heart rate instantly increased by twenty beats per minute—then ten more as I took in the disapproving look on her face.

"Isabella Stanford?" she asked, her eyes raking up and down my five-foot-ten frame. I suddenly felt ashamed, not just of my relatively disheveled appearance, just out of the shower, but of my height. All my life people had tried to persuade me that I should feel grateful to be tall, but I had always wanted to be petite. Grass is always greener, of course, but my height had definitely limited my luxury prospects on SA—no one could deny that.

"Yes?" I said, already feeling defensive.

"I'm Maria," the nurse replied. "I'm here to do your screening for the research program you signed up for."

"I know," I said lamely. "I was... I guess I'm running late?" I swallowed hard, looking at her severe face, then stood aside to let her brush past me and into my apartment.

"That's alright," she said, though she clearly didn't feel that way. "You can go ahead and take off your clothes."

CHAPTER 2

 sabella

"What?" I asked, genuinely confused. "Oh, you mean for my blood pressure? I can just roll up my sleeve, right?"

I showed Maria that my arm would be free, though I couldn't remember a medical professional having had trouble with a short-sleeved shirt before.

"No," said Maria, frowning. "Everything. You can keep your panties on for now, but I'll need you to take them down when I do the arousal check and install your sensor."

"The *what*? And... *install* my... what?" I felt like my eyes would pop out of my head.

Maria shook her head, blowing a snort of frustration through her nostrils. "Honey, you didn't read the agreement, did you?"

My cheeks went from cool to furnace-hot in a millisecond. "I did," I lied. "But… you know… that legal language. I couldn't…"

My voice trailed off as I saw that the nurse had started to tap things on the tablet she had produced from her bag. She held it up and turned it to me. From the scroll bar on the right-hand side of the screen I could see that this section must be two pages into the agreement, if that. My cheeks only got hotter as I read.

I agree to comply with the instructions of the medical professional assigned to carry out my screening examination. I acknowledge that this examination concerns my sexual health and that therefore I will be required to remove all my clothing, and to undergo sexual stimulation by the screener. I agree to the installation on my person of a monitoring sensor, and to the use by Selecta of the data from that sensor.

"Couldn't get much clearer than that, could it?" Maria asked when she'd given me thirty seconds to take it in.

I raised my eyes to hers, and I felt regret building in my body, a sob beginning in my chest. I fought it off, pushed it down, and chose defiance instead.

"Well," I said, "I mean… it will never hold up in court, right?" I wrinkled my nose and looked at Maria as scornfully as I could.

"No," she agreed with a sigh. She withdrew the tablet and turned it to herself. She began tapping. "At least I get paid whether or not you go through with it, honey. Can't say the same for you."

"Wait!" I said. "What are you doing?"

She looked up with raised eyebrows. "I'm telling Selecta that you've broken the agreement."

"And…"

The dark brows knit themselves into a frown. "And what do you think, Isabella? That lovely stipend you got this morning is going bye-bye."

Again sorrow threatened to seize control, and again I forced it down and set my face into as hard an expression as I could manage. Maria clearly had some kind of chip on her shoulder about Selecta Arrangements girls, I thought. She obviously took some pleasure in the thought of ripping the lifeline I had managed to secure out of my hands.

A zillion thoughts whirled in my brain.

I should have known.

Selecta was that kind of company. I should have understood that something intensely embarrassing, even invasive and degrading, would be involved. At the same time, in order to continue walking the edge of what society would accept, I knew that Selecta also scrupulously complied with the law—and with basic ethics—in the area of consent. They certainly put young women in difficult positions in their leveraging of traditional gender roles, but those positions came from society and not from Selecta's exploitation of them.

I need the money. I need the money so bad.

"Wait," I said again, hearing how much less certain my voice had become.

Maria looked up; her eyebrows once again raised. Her finger hovered over a button on her tablet screen, and I felt certain that the next tap she made would seize back the money—all the money—from my account.

"I'll..." my voice started out weak, but I put rebellious scorn into it as I continued. "What the hell. I'll do it."

A tiny smile turned up the left corner of the nurse's mouth. I felt another surge of heat to my face as I had the uncomfortable thought that she had gone through precisely this decision-making process with hundreds of women—then stood watching as they all removed their clothing, knowing the humiliating consequences to come.

Knowing but also not knowing. My heart quailed at the thought of what the *arousal check* might involve.

Maria looked down and tapped a different button on her screen from the one she had seemed about to tap. She raised her eyes to look into my blushing face.

"May I sit down?" she asked. "I'll just get my stethoscope and blood pressure cuff, and then we can get started once you have your clothes off."

My forehead creased, and I bit my lip, but with a concerted effort I managed to readjust my expression to hard neutrality.

"Okay," I told her and turned my back.

Once I had faced away from Maria, I could let my face go. I chewed the inside of my cheek as I pulled my t-shirt over my head and dropped it to the sofa. Behind me, I heard the nurse sit in the armchair next to the window, and then I heard the rustling of her getting things out of the bag.

"You're five foot nine?" she asked.

I felt my mouth twist to the side, as I unbuttoned my jeans.

"Ten," I said.

"And your scale tells me you weigh 175 or so," she said.

I had to bite my lip to keep a sound of protest—or of shame—from escaping at her peremptory, disapproving tone. To have her say that, just as I pulled down my jeans to reveal my backside and its mortifying expansion over the past two years or so, made me want to sink into the floor.

To stay in good standing in the Selecta Arrangements program, associate members had to weigh themselves every morning. Just one of those little humiliations that had become second nature to me, so much so that I didn't even look at the number. I didn't think 175 was that bad, really, but Maria clearly didn't see it that way.

"So you know," she said, "that's just a bit overweight according to your BMI. You should think about adjusting your diet."

My jaw dropped, and I had to keep myself from whirling around to face her with some wounded retort. To my horror, tears leaked from the corner of my eyes.

"I know," I said, as casually as I could. "I'm trying to watch my diet."

Slowly, I straightened up, willing my hands to stay by my sides. I refused to give this woman the satisfaction of seeing how badly she had embarrassed me—how thoroughly she had invoked the childish modesty I thought I had left behind years ago, around the time I had started having sex with a man who gave me an allowance.

"It gets harder as you get older," Maria said. Her voice sounded sympathetic.

I turned, keeping my hands at my side, looking the nurse in the eye so she could see what I hoped looked like a jaded expression.

The expression on the older woman's face, though, made me look down at my feet: she might *sound* sympathetic, but her face looked one hundred percent judgmental—or much, much worse... patronizing. I almost commented on her own weight, which did *not* look to be in the healthy BMI range.

Then I thought of what Maria's response might be—*Well, honey, I don't fuck for money, do I?*—and I felt my nose twitch with the effort to keep the blush away.

"Have a seat on the sofa," she told me. With renewed effort, I put a simpering smile on my face and obeyed, and for the next five minutes Maria became all business, and despite my near-nakedness the exam seemed to settle down into something like normality.

Blood pressure 120 over 90. Fine. Whatever they listened for when they put the cold end of the stethoscope all over you and told you to breathe. Fine. Hammer on the knee made my leg kick. Wonderful.

"You'll have a full gynecological workup at the research facility," Maria told me, as she put the cuff, the stethoscope, and the funny rubber hammer back into her bag. "If you're accepted. It's looking fine so far, but I'm afraid the embarrassing part is about to start. You should probably get a towel from the bathroom to put on the sofa."

To my dismay, my jaw dropped once again. "Why?" I asked, despite my best effort to bite my tongue over the monosyllable.

Maria's lips pursed with what looked like disgust.

"Isabella, you were offered a place in this program because you're very likely to experience a sort of arousal Selecta's very interested in right now, in experienced associate members of their Selecta Arrangements program. If you do experience that level of arousal, it

could get a little messy—messier than when you masturbate, if you masturbate."

My breathing had become rapid and shallow as I stared at
the nurse. She held my gaze steadily, her lips still pursed,
her eyebrows rising to suggest that I should get on with
the humiliation.

"I…" I tried. "I don't…"

"I know you don't, honey," Maria replied. "That's part of
the point."

I turned and fled, more or less, to the bathroom, feeling
the heat surge into my cheeks and down my neck.

I took all the time I thought I could choosing a towel
before the horrible nurse might come looking for me.
With my hands running over the terry cloth, not really
feeling its softness at all, I tried to figure out what I could
possibly have meant to say, after *don't*.

I don't get that aroused? True. Sex was fine. I liked that I
could use it to keep nice men supporting me and wanting
to see me. I didn't enjoy thinking about it very much,
because it didn't feel fantastic to put out in order to eat
out—as some of the girls on the Selecta Arrangements
forums put it.

One of the things the program got right—as I agreed with
the other knowledgeable girls on the forums—was
making lube one of the fully-subsidized items in an SA
girl's shopping. I got all the lube I needed delivered
monthly, and it helped make the sex feel… fine. Some

girls in SA actually didn't like sex; I knew that, and I felt thankful I didn't have that problem. Sex felt good, but not, I had to confess, great.

I don't...

I don't... play with myself? Also true.

I hadn't ever seen the point, really. Why make yourself feel embarrassed that way? When I saw in videos what orgasm supposedly looked like, my cheeks got hot, and if I was alone I fast forwarded. The loss of control, especially over your face... What amount of pleasure could make that worth it, I always wondered.

The men I'd slept with—my one real boyfriend, if he could be called that, from the time before Selecta Arrangements, and my sponsors—had asked about my orgasms or lack of them. I had told them that I didn't think I could and fucking felt fine, and not to worry. They had seemed grateful for the reassurance, and they had happily come inside my pussy, while I carefully closed my eyes so I wouldn't have to see their silly faces.

I chewed on the inside of my cheek as I chose a towel at last and turned to go back to whatever humiliation awaited me in the living room. I didn't have any idea whether I hoped this stupid nurse would discover something in me that I didn't know had been there—something that would let me into this program, despite the shame involved—or if I hoped it would turn out Selecta had made a mistake.

If they'd made a mistake, would they at least let me keep the month of luxury allowance they had already put in my account, instead of ripping it away?

"You can put the towel down on the sofa," Maria told me. "Then go ahead and take off your panties for me, please, and sit right on the towel."

CHAPTER 3

sabella

I guess I thought that I couldn't blush any hotter when the nurse instructed me to get the towel in the first place, but taking down my underwear in front of her made it clear I had several degrees Fahrenheit to go in my burning cheeks. With a level of self-consciousness that felt like not just Maria the nurse but a live studio audience was watching me, I fixed my gaze on the white terrycloth and hooked my thumbs into the waistband of the pink cotton panties.

They took only a moment to pull down and off and to drop onto the sofa, but the ungainly action seemed to go on forever. Then I felt another surge of warmth as I tried to adjust the way the cotton fell so that Maria wouldn't be able to see the gusset of the panties. I knew I had just put them on and there couldn't be anything embarrassing for her to see there, but my modest instincts prevailed just the same. It made me feel even more awkward and mortified when I realized it would probably look to Maria like I had something to hide—and what the fuck could I possibly be hiding that a nurse would find shameful?

That was when I suddenly realized that if I hadn't just taken off the cotton panties, I might indeed have had something to conceal. To my surprised distress, I felt the warmth of the blush in my cheeks down *there* as well.

Had something about this humiliating situation... stirred me, that way? My mind recoiled from the idea as if I had just seen a snake in the middle of the path on a hike in the woods. My hands drifted to my lap, as if the heat there, and even the possible wetness, might become visible to Maria.

"You can go ahead and sit down," she repeated from behind me. "Then I'm going to need you to raise your knees and hold them open for me."

Oh God. No, please.

The nurse's terrible words—the kind of thing no gynecologist, and none of my lovers, even, had ever said—had just made me *clench* down there.

Sure, at the doctor's office for your pelvic exam, you put your feet in the stirrups. And sex felt more comfortable with your knees raised... but that felt very different. The heat built in my face as I thought about my last sponsor, and how he had always wanted the light on for sex. That had felt good, because I knew it meant he thought I was hot—though it always led to a little insecurity when I confronted myself in the bathroom mirror the next morning.

But… when you started having sex, you were kissing, and then you rolled onto your back to tell him you were ready… and of course you'd just gone to the bathroom discreetly to apply the lube and take off your panties so you felt kind of sexy… and your legs just opened a little and he smiled when his experienced fingers discovered you had no underwear on.

And maybe he said, "So nice and smooth," and you bit your lip and felt a bit of a blush, and he got undressed, and *then* you spread your legs a little more so he could get between them… and *after that* you raised your knees so he could get into you.

I realized, as I looked at the towel, that several seconds had gone by while I had gotten lost in thinking about sex. A new flare of heat shot through my body, all the way through my body, so strong and so full of an unfamiliar, mortifying kind of arousal that a sob rose into my throat and I had to conceal it with a fake cough.

Why had I started to think about sex like that? I *never* thought about sex. I did it naturally. I let it happen. My first boyfriend had had a reasonable amount of experience, so he had helped me with my initial awkwardness— he had even known about lube. With my sponsors, well, they had both been married and divorced, so the bedroom had just seemed… natural.

Thinking about it… didn't seem natural. But something about what the awful nurse had just said had somehow made me—*forced* me, it felt like—to think about what it meant to spread my legs and raise my knees.

"Honey," Maria said from behind me, her voice sounding truly sympathetic, "I can give you another minute, but if you don't follow my instructions, I have to tell Selecta, and they'll take the money back. But if it helps, about a quarter of the girls accepted to this research program don't go through with the screening, so you shouldn't feel too bad about it."

My forehead creased deeply. Along with the unwelcome sexual feeling, the nurse's words seemed to hit at my pride as well as my wallet. Part of me wanted to throw Maria out of my apartment, give back the money, put my clothes on and start looking for economy men grateful to date me and ready to make a commitment if they could keep fucking me.

Another part of me wanted to turn to her in tears, begging for mercy, pouring out my heart about being thirty years old and having no future. What good would that do, though?

A coldly rational thought took shape in my mind, though. I should show Maria that I just didn't fucking care. I had three years of experience in Selecta Arrangements. I had had two moderate sponsors who had greatly enjoyed fucking me. Why should spreading my legs and raising my knees for an exam matter to me?

Alongside that idea, from deeper inside me—so deep it felt like something that came from my body itself—arose an urge that I pushed back hard, but not before it had made me start to sit down. For a moment, I felt completely shameless, and I didn't stop to think—I didn't *want* to think. I wanted to show my pussy to the nurse.

I didn't know why, and I forced myself not to care why, because it all seemed to work together. I could keep the money, and I could do the terribly naughty thing that made my knees suddenly seem wobbly under me.

I sat on the towel, turning so that I could see Maria again. The sight of what she had gotten out of her bag—the one thing she had put on the coffee table and the other thing she held in her hand—made the still-modest part of me regret my compliance instantly. My jaw dropped and my eyes went wide.

On the table was something I had enough experience on the net to know was a vibrator. The white wand kind— the kind that made girls scream in funny videos that got my face hot.

In the nurse's hand, a mirror. A simple hand mirror of the sort that always seemed old-fashioned to me, though this one was made of white plastic and clearly represented the latest model. Wildly, I thought about how Maria could have taken a picture on her handheld and then shown it to me, but how that wouldn't have had the directness, the simplicity, or it seemed to me the sheer degradation of the hand mirror.

She saw me gazing at it in horror. She smiled gently.

"You've never had a really good look, have you?" she asked.

My lips still parted, I shook my head. I knew how very pink my cheeks had gotten, and that made the embarrassment even worse.

"Go ahead and lift your knees. You can put your feet on the coffee table."

A moment ago, I had wanted to show her my pussy. Why did it seem so shameful—the thought of looking at it myself?

Because it... Because I...

Because I want to. It's naughty, but I want to look.

Want. Wanton.

"I'm..." I whispered, as much to myself as to Maria. "I'm *thirty*."

Her smile got a little wider.

"You mean you think you're too old to be finding out what arouses you, honey?" she asked, in her sympathetic voice.

I bit my lip. I had a choice to make, I suddenly realized. I made it: defiance and refusal. Instead of accepting the nurse's patronizing kindness, I decided to maintain the tough skin I had developed in Selecta Arrangements, where rejection practically represented a way of life. It had taken me countless dates to find my moderate sponsors. Some of them I had passed on; much more often, the wealthy man had passed on me.

"No," I said coldly, lying and thrusting the lie into my own heart as well, telling my body, my pussy, that it was being stupid. "Sorry. I mean that I'm too old to be treated this way."

Standing over me, the mirror in her hand like a weapon, Maria nodded. The smile vanished from her face.

"Got it. Put your feet on the coffee table, please. This is an important part of the exam. I'm going to install your sensor, and then I'm going to use the vibrator to test it, as well as to check your arousal cycle."

I twisted my mouth to the side, buying fully into my choice to comply only with as much evident scorn as I could muster.

"Whatever," I told her.

To my distress, Maria seemed to have to ward off a laugh, turning it into a slight cough. She raised her eyebrows, clearly telling me to get on with it.

Sluggishly, I did. I pulled my knees up and put my feet on the coffee table. I felt the cool air of the room against my private parts, and I forced myself to look out the picture window instead of at the nurse. I tried to push away the very knowledge of my nakedness and thought about the clouds.

Maria clearly had no intention of letting me forget, however. I had no idea what the purpose of the research program I had signed up for even was, I realized to my dismay, and with every passing moment of this exam it seemed like it must involve something absolutely mortifying. Maria seemed resolved to make it all as humiliating as possible, at any rate.

"I need you to look in the mirror, Isabella," she said sternly. "Your vulva is an important part of you."

Ugh, that word. For some reason it seemed so much dirtier even than *pussy*. I fought back the tears of stress that threatened to well up in the corners of my eyes. With as much of a *whatever* expression as I could put on my face, I turned my eyes to see that the nurse had thrust the mirror between my thighs. In it... I bit my lip... I could see everything.

My fists clenched into little balls along my naked hips.

Everything: the pout of my pussy, its pale, thick outer lips and the delicate pink of the inner ones. The complex folds on top, where my clit lay hidden. My clit, where I didn't really have all that much feeling, I thought, in comparison to the way I'd read I should, and other girls described. One of my sponsors had tried earnestly to make me come for a while, a few times, and it had made me think my clit lacked some nerve endings.

I felt my forehead crease as that idea suddenly seemed less likely, because as I looked at myself, my pussy and my wrinkly little anus, I felt a tingle there even at the movement of the air caused by Maria's mirror.

I'm thirty. I almost whispered it again in disbelief and protest.

I'm thirty and she shouldn't treat me like this, I insisted to myself. *That's what it is.*

Maria had shifted the mirror to her left hand and reached her right index finger down to a little card she had put on the coffee table alongside the vibrator.

"I have the sensor on my finger now," she told me. "It's nearly invisible. I'm going to touch you now, between your vagina and your anus, and you'll feel a little itch—not pain, really—as the sensor installs itself."

CHAPTER 4

 arl

I studied the data stream coming from the sensor the nurse was about to install on Isabella Stanford's vulva. If the girl had intrigued me before—from the moment I had gotten the email alert about newcomers to the new Selecta program for thirty-year-olds and looked through the pictures—she positively interested me now. Her reactions to the screening exam seemed an inextricable mixture of embarrassment, arousal, alarm, and—best of all—a piquant hint of defiance.

Grit and spirit, I couldn't help thinking. I didn't have any real expertise in interpreting the data Selecta fed men in my position, members of Selecta Arrangements who paid a pretty extra penny to get "Diamond" level of service—or who, like me, had that level comped to them thanks to special services to Selecta. I had watched a few young women's feeds, though, and I could tell from experience that despite herself, Isabella had gotten at least as turned on spreading her legs for the nurse as I had in watching her display her utterly gorgeous, neatly shaved pussy.

The data feed came with a video feed direct from Isabella's apartment. It had turned on, I guessed, the moment she signed the agreement with the research program. I had opened it when the alert came in that a new subject's screening exam had begun.

I had a particular interest in this program because I'd had an important hand in designing it. I didn't work for Selecta, though the megacorp had expressed an interest in buying my small but extremely lucrative company. The reason for all the money coming in lay in exactly the same quarter as my interest in Isabella: a piece of proprietary biodigital code I had written, which served as the foundation of the RELM program Isabella would soon—it seemed very likely, judging from the way she looked at the vibrator on her coffee table—join.

RELM: *Romance Enhancement for Legacy Members.* The Selecta docs had used my code to put something very special into the pharmaceutical concoction Isabella would probably start taking in just a few hours. Whatever that secret sauce might be, it belonged to the megacorp's carefully guarded, truly extraordinary arsenal of psychosexual knowledge and technique. What those guys didn't know about human sexuality, I sometimes thought, couldn't fill a pamphlet, let alone a book—and the pamphlet wouldn't even be worth reading.

I looked into Isabella's eyes on the video feed from a camera that the Selecta-owned builders of her apartment had presumably installed in an upper corner of her living room. I saw her struggle when, from offscreen over the excellent audio feed, a loud, almost angry buzzing began to fill the air. Isabella's eyes went wide and, on her data feed, the line that compiled all the data Selecta had about her current level of sexual arousal, jumped like a rabbit on a pogo stick.

I zoomed out to see Maria Renato—a label on the video helpfully told me the nurse's name—begin to bring the vibrator near Isabella's sweet, cringing pussy.

Isabella

I hadn't thought the vibrator would be so loud. I hadn't thought it *could* be so loud. How could something that looked like my immersion blender—which only made a whirring sort of noise, in comparison—sound like that?

"Put your hands under your thighs," Maria instructed.

My lips parted and my eyes went wide. With what felt like a terrible effort, I set my face into a mask of indifference —or as near as I could manage.

Who cares? I don't... I don't care... I don't play with myself because what's the point?

I made my hands do as the nurse had instructed. I tried not to think about it—I had no idea... made myself have no idea, why she had told me to do that.

In her hand, the wand seemed to have an angry life of its own. The noise threatened to make me feel faint as I watched it, the vibrations of the big white knob at its end making the slightly pebbled surface look blurry and indistinct.

"Spread your labia a little, Isabella. I need you to feel exposed." Maria's voice had taken on a strange, imperious tone that seemed to create a new effect in me—somewhere deep inside that I found very disquieting.

The discomfort helped me set my face into a scornful look. I knit my brows and narrowed my eyes and said, "Why?" in a tone that came to my ears as satisfyingly defiant.

"The screening for this program," she replied, inclining her chin to emphasize the authority she had so dismayingly gained over me through the agreement I probably should have read more carefully, "involves seeing whether you can be put into a certain psychosexual state that you probably haven't experienced before, and—if you *can* be put there—seeing what effect it has on you."

I swallowed hard, the action completely involuntary. I kept the sneer on my face, but at the back of my mind something had started to come into focus, and I didn't like the shape of it at all.

"I don't understand," I said, my voice trying to stay flat in tone but to my distress taking on a pleading sound.

"I'm afraid you're not supposed to, honey. Do as I say, please. Spread your labia for me. Show me your vagina."

My breath caught in my throat as my fingers started to obey, at the behest not of my conscious mind so much as the thing in the back of it, the... the...

Wanton curiosity. The phrase drifted through my brain. It made my hips jerk against the hands I held underneath my backside, clutching and opening. It made my face flinch.

It brought heat, down there where my fingertips had done as Maria commanded, and shown her the sheath where my lovers had put their cocks, where I had lubed myself for their pleasure and my comfort.

To enjoy themselves without truly pleasuring me, despite— sometimes, anyway—their best efforts.

If a man had been there, in my apartment, his hard penis ready for me, the lack of lube wouldn't have posed a problem, I suddenly realized. My cheeks flushed as hot as a furnace.

The buzzing knob came so close. I couldn't take my eyes off it, except that my gaze also had to flick to the nurse's intent, impassive face, as if to confirm that Maria's attention was, as I feared and couldn't help hoping, fixed on my pussy.

It's too low, I thought. The vibrator wouldn't touch me where I needed it the most—and where I dreaded it the most, where my clit, still hidden in its wrinkly hood, tingled so terribly I had to bite my lip. The knob moved slowly not in that direction, but toward the hole, lower down, as if its monstrous girth could enter me there. I had an ache inside, too, and I desperately wanted something inside—but not the huge wand.

"Please," I whispered, but Maria held the buzzing knob so close now that I thought I could feel the way it moved the air itself against the entrance to my vagina. My fingers, holding myself down there, trembled terribly, and I couldn't help opening myself even more despite the degradation of it and the panic that filled my chest at the thought of what it would feel like when the nurse finally pressed the device against my most intimate places.

Maria spoke slowly and deliberately. "I want you to think about your body," she said.

My jaw went slack and my breath came in little pants. I felt my forehead crease very deeply as I looked up from the vibrator into the nurse's face again.

"What?" I asked. I had understood her words, of course, but if I wasn't thinking about my body right now, what the fuck was I thinking about?

"I want you to imagine that your body is different."

35

I still had no idea what she meant, really, but her words—just one of them, really... *different*—made my heart race even more than it already was. My eyes went from Maria's face to the vibrator, and between the two I saw her other hand reaching toward my chest.

"Wh—" I started, intending to say, *What are you doing?* but the nurse's hand made that perfectly clear a moment later when her fingers began to fondle my tiny breasts.

"Imagine you have big breasts, Isabella. D cups. And wide hips. Imagine you have a classic hourglass figure, and that that's exactly what your husband wants."

Then she touched the knob of the vibrator to my pussy, and she started to move it gradually upward, toward my clit, and I cried out as if she had struck me, and I started to come.

I couldn't think, I could only feel, and I could only watch the pictures Maria had put in my head. As the waves of pleasure crashed through my body, with my very first orgasm, I sobbed as much at the way my brain responded as at the sheer excess of physical delight the vibrator forced on me.

I saw it. I saw myself, and I saw my nonexistent husband.

My boyish figure, of which I had always felt a little ashamed, transformed into a busty, curvy shape. I had a lacy red babydoll nightgown on. My hubby had told me to put it on, and to wait for him, in bed... no, not in bed—in the living room... in the living room, where a neighbor might be able to look into the big suburban picture window and see the young wife in her lingerie...

On my knees, in front of his armchair, waiting to...

Waiting to...

"Oh God," I sobbed, as I came again. I had my eyes closed so I could see the hot young wife... how old?

Eighteen... only eighteen... barely legal...

The shame and the need flowed through me. My body bucked against the sofa cushions. Beneath my bottom, my fingers clutched at the place where my tight little cheeks became my slim thighs.

Not like the young wife in the images Maria had given me.

She spoke again, and every word seemed to prolong the second orgasm of my life, until I could hardly bear it.

"You were naughty," the nurse said. "Your husband told you to get ready for a spanking. When he comes home, he's going to give it to you."

Oh no. The knob of the vibrator moved up to my clit, and I screamed, writhing against my own fingers as I clutched my bottom cheeks in helpless response to Maria's mortifying words.

Over his knee... punished... before I have to...

My handsome, older husband... sitting in his chair, pulling me across his lap...

His hand, spanking me so hard for my wanton curiosity... for having such big breasts and such full hips... for wearing the red nightgown he had told me to wear... for needing his hardness inside my greedy young pussy so very badly.

Me, crying out... begging him to stop spanking my big, round bottom...

Making me kneel, opening his fly, taking it out... his huge, hard cock.

I had never—none of my lovers had made me—but my commanding husband would... my mouth, forced down... the rigid penis inside, making me serve my master's pleasure...

Way up high, off in the stratosphere of my mind where an observer still seemed to sit in judgment despite my having ignored all her opinions for the last five minutes or so, I wondered what the fuck Maria's degrading words had done to me. Sure, I thought, like so many women, I had a touch of dysmorphia, of not feeling like I had the body I really wanted.

Now, at thirty, it seemed natural that I should look with envy at hourglass-shaped women who could wear clothes I never could... And who you couldn't help but fantasize might leverage their bodies into suburban lifestyles with rich older men. But it had never occurred to me that I might have lurking in my unconscious some humiliating sexual feeling about it.

For a moment I tried to resist, tried to tense my body against the pleasure. I tried thinking about... about... traffic... trucks...

Trucks my handsome husband would drive, parking outside his house, knowing I was inside waiting for my spanking.

"Oh, please," I whimpered, feeling a third climax begin to build inside me, the biggest of them all.

I heard a click, somewhere off in the distance, and the buzzing stopped. I gave a little wail because the pleasure had stopped too.

"Get your clothes back on," Maria said calmly. "I'm going to take you to the research center. You've been accepted into the program."

sabella

The van waiting in the garage of my building brought me and Maria to a clinic only a few blocks away. Before the van drove the ramp into the vast basement parking area, I managed to get a look out the window, up into the sky between the skyscrapers.

"Is this the Selecta building?" I asked Maria, frowning. "I thought we'd be going to a clinic or something."

"Oh, there's a clinic in here. There are five of them, I think, all working on different projects," she told me. "Your program uses research from all of them, if I'm not mistaken."

The van had pulled up to a bank of elevators behind glass doors. I saw two security guards standing outside there, and one of them walked up to the door of the van practically before we had stopped moving. He opened it and looked straight at me.

Maria had let me put on my clothes again, obviously, but I felt like the burly guard could see through them, somehow. He didn't mentally undress me—I had gotten used to that look on a man's face from many dates with potential sponsors. No, the guard looked at me as if my jeans and t-shirt didn't matter—as if here in the Selecta building, the tallest skyscraper on the east coast, I was in some fundamental way naked whether they had allowed me clothing or not. If I had something on, I might just as easily be told to take it off, and...

Made use of.

Ugh. I felt the strange, new arousal rouse itself again. *Wanton curiosity.*

What the fuck.

I steered my mind away from the little story that had somehow floated into my brain, about a security guard who told a thirty-year-old to take her clothes off so that he could push her face against a glass door and get his hard cock into her from behind. I pushed on my thoughts —it really felt like that, like trying to drive them back from filthy, dangerous ground.

I thought about the sky outside between the buildings, the glimpse of the huge letters way up there that read SELECTA.

You can trust SELECTA. Their hilarious slogan, dating from the time of the corporate laws. Everyone made fun of it on the Selecta Arrangements forums. And yet it had an essential truth, everyone also seemed to admit. I remembered that a recent poll had shown that the public trusted Selecta more than the government by something like twenty points. You couldn't ever tell what the mega-corps intended—they had to keep their secrets from the competition, after all—but you could trust them to do everything in their power to keep their clients happy.

As I took the security guard's huge hand and let him help me out of the van, I swallowed hard. Selecta's clients didn't include me, really, did they? My sponsors, yes—the actual members of Selecta Arrangements, to whom associate members like me were… well… offered.

Maria followed me. Inside the little elevator lobby, the other guard pressed the down button, and the doors of one of the elevators glided open.

"Down?" I asked, a little surprised that the elevators even had that button, since it had seemed like the van had descended as far as the garage could take us.

"Mm-hmm," Maria responded, gesturing to me with an ushering movement it seemed my body had to obey, though my heart rate had begun to rise drastically.

Offered. And this research program…

Inside the elevator, there were buttons for L, P1, P2, and *PRODUCT DEVELOPMENT.*

Maria pressed the one for Product Development.

I felt my face scrunch into a mask of confusion as my cheeks got hot. I bit my tongue because I knew it would do no good to ask about the phrase. I was the product. I had signed up to help them develop *me*.

Into what? Into something more... desirable?

I felt my breathing start to speed up. The guard had stepped into the elevator after us—the one who had looked at me like I had no clothes on. His huge back loomed in front of me as the elevator doors closed.

Maria looked sharply over at me. Turning my eyes to her and trying to keep them impassive despite everything, I could see genuine surprise in her face—as if she hadn't expected me to put it together, and that my clear signs of a beginning panic attack represented, in her book, proof of intelligence.

Put it together: the different body... the big breasts... a dominant husband...

PRODUCT DEVELOPMENT.

The sign that confronted us as soon as the elevator doors opened after a downward trip of five minutes said the same thing, but in cheerful red letters that matched the much-too-familiar corporate font of Selecta.

A man in a white lab coat over a shirt and tie stood there. To my distress, I found my feet wouldn't move, though I tried to do the obvious, natural thing and exit the elevator —not because I had any real desire to meet the doctor but because I really needed more time to figure out whether I had made an unbelievably big mistake.

"Time to get off," Maria said beside me.

My hands clenched into fists at my side. My knees felt wobbly.

"Joe," the nurse said, without apparent surprise or annoyance, "could you help Isabella, please?"

The big guard turned to me, a slight smile on his face.

"Let's not keep the doctor waiting," he said in an impossibly deep voice.

I looked up into his eyes, and instinctively my hands moved in front of my body. Instead of taking a step forward, I took one back, to bring myself up against the rear wall of the elevator.

Now Maria did sigh. The guard's—Joe's—face became annoyed.

"I—," I said. "I don't—"

The guard stepped forward and reached for me. My eyes went to the doctor, who had a tablet in his hands, on which he had started to type, as if taking notes on my reluctance. My body seemed to want to go in three different directions, but when Joe's enormous hand took hold of my elbow and I felt his massive strength, my limbs decided the matter for me. I started to struggle wildly but futilely against him.

He picked me up as if I weighed nothing at all. I kicked at him but to my dismay he clearly had a lot of experience in conveying reluctant young women where Selecta wanted them to go. As I twisted my head around in a desperate struggle to gain some purchase on the huge masculine body so effortlessly manhandling mine, I caught sight of the doctor again.

He had one eye on his tablet and the other on me; I saw him glance up and then down again. My face burned as I realized he must be looking at real-time data coming from the sensor between my legs...inside my panties, where a heat to match the blush on my face suddenly rose to a raging, mortifying level.

I realized it had started to build down there since the moment I had read the words PRODUCT DEVELOP-MENT next to the elevator button and connected them to what Maria had told me to think about while...

I felt my face twist into a sob, and I couldn't keep it away. The sense memory of what the nurse had done to me on the sofa in my apartment came flooding back. I kept trying to get away from Joe as he hauled me through the elevator doors at last, but my struggle had become almost perfunctory because my brain had come much more strongly under the influence of horror—horror at the intent look on the doctor's face, the little smile, not of enjoyment but of... satisfaction. I could see in the eyes that still flicked up and down from the tablet to me that my reluctance, my resistance, my rebellion... they all looked to him like the commonplace reactions of a thirty-year-old woman to her induction into a research program that clearly had the goal of turning her into a better product.

"This is Isabella Stanford," Maria told him from slightly behind where Joe had taken a stand in the little elevator lobby about a yard from the doctor.

"Isabella Stanford," he said, finally looking into my eyes, nodding slightly, "I'm afraid we have rules here, and one of them is that you do as you're told by the medical professionals in charge of the program."

I stopped my feeble struggles as my heart started to thud much harder in my chest than even the effort of resistance had made it beat. My eyes widened and my jaw went slack. I couldn't mistake his meaning, though for a split second I tried very, very hard.

Selecta, as every girl who read the Selecta Arrangements forums with any care at all knew, endorsed traditional family discipline. Maria had included it in her terrible little story about me with a different body and a dominant husband.

"No," I croaked, though I wanted to yell it. "You... you can't!"

The doctor glanced over at Maria. "She's just as smart as her profile says, isn't she? A shame a young woman like her didn't get the chance at a real education."

"What?" I demanded. "I have a fine—"

He interrupted me, addressing the guard. "Take her to the discipline room, please, Joe. Just a hand spanking for her first lesson."

"Of course, Dr. Hethcote," Joe replied in that voice that seemed to rumble through my body as well as his. "On her bare butt?"

My breath came raggedly between my lips as I watched the doctor consider his answer. He frowned, looking down at his tablet. Then he looked at me and said, "Yes, definitely."

I shook my head, my lips moving with words I couldn't find, utter panic filling my chest, my belly.

"Isabella, you need to learn obedience as soon as possible," he said, in a serious, patronizing voice. "I can see that the best way is to start you off with your bottom bare over Joe's knee."

He turned toward the one door leading out of the lobby and waved the ID on a lanyard around his neck. It clicked and Dr. Hethcote opened it outward while Joe began to move in that direction.

Then I started to struggle for real again, but my limbs had started to tire to my disgust. Even if I had been twice as strong, I knew I could never have gotten out of the enormous guard's grip, though. He just put me over his shoulder, literally like a sack of potatoes.

Worse, Maria followed us, a put-upon look on her face as she regarded me in my horribly ungainly position. I had raised my fists as Joe carried me through the door, intending to hit the back of the guard if only to show that I wouldn't give in. The expression on the nurse's face stopped me though, and I merely closed my eyes and sobbed.

"You c—can't," I choked, again wishing I could scream it.

Dr. Hethcote had come through the door now too, and it had begun to close behind him. As he walked, he still looked down at the tablet, obviously following every little moment of data that came from between my legs.

Another sob burst from me and I closed my eyes, scrunching them shut as hard as I could. This couldn't really be happening, could it?

I felt Joe change directions abruptly, turning a corner, and I opened my eyes, which had started to leak profusely with tears of rage and humiliation, to see that we had entered the discipline room.

"Oh no," I whispered, my voice just a weak plea now as I took in the contents of the room. "No... you have to let me go."

CHAPTER 6

 *sabella*

"Try to relax, Isabella," said Dr. Hethcote as he stepped through the door and closed it behind him with a metallic thunk that told me the room was almost certainly sound-proofed. "I know how hard that sounds, but you'd have to be a very naughty girl to earn a lesson from most of what you see on that rack."

Paddles—leather ones and wooden ones. Straps, some long and flexible looking, others shorter and stiff.

My breathing sped up even further.

Canes. Long and thin.

But the doctor seemed to have developed the impression that the rack had terrified me the most. Frankly, the two benches near it, close to the far wall of the rather sizable room, which also to my dismay featured a mirror along the whole length of another wall, horrified me more. They had *restraints* on them, and though I tried not to let my imagination go there, I understood immediately how you would put two young women over them, with their faces turned toward the mirror.

The benches, however, didn't represent the most frightening thing in the room, for me at that moment anyway.

No, that title was reserved for the simple high-backed chair toward which Joe had started to carry me, beginning to turn as he all too clearly prepared to take me off his shoulder and sit down in it. There didn't seem to exist any way I could stop my mind from exploring the possibilities of what would happen when we got there—although only one of those potential outcomes, the worst possible one, had any likelihood of coming true.

"No... please, no," I begged. My ability to raise my voice had come back to me, over Joe's shoulder, but though I also did start to beat at the guard's brawny back with my fists, I sounded terribly weak, terribly desperate. I felt weak too. Not only had I gotten tired in my struggles but the sheer strength of Joe's frame made my efforts seem much punier in comparison.

I caught sight of Dr. Hethcote again. I looked him in the face, expecting him to utter some reassurance that it wouldn't hurt very much—or even some silly paternalistic pronouncement like, "This is going to hurt me more than it hurts you." He merely looked back at me with a tight little smile and then looked down at his tablet.

Joe showed again that he had done this many times. The movement with which he lifted me from his shoulder and set me on the industrial-gray carpeted floor, sitting in the old-fashioned rail-back chair at the same time and even beginning to pull me down over his enormous thigh happened in what seemed like a nanosecond.

I flailed, feeling paradoxically that if I had managed to free myself even a millimeter from the guard's grasp, I would almost certainly have ended up in a heap on the floor, but unable now to keep from struggling. My flight reflex had taken over, rising in the sheer panic created by the guard's dominant presence and the absolute inevitability that I would now receive the very first spanking of my life.

A wailing cry burst from my lips as he pulled me down over his knee. I looked up to see that Maria had come to stand in front of me, while Dr. Hethcote had taken a position to my side and squarely in front of the chair and the seated Joe. For a moment I tried to put an impassive, uncaring look on my face, but then the guard shifted a bit on the seat of the chair, using his iron grip around my waist to pull me toward him, and I couldn't keep down the sob of fear that rose in my chest.

"You've never been truly punished in your life, have you, Isabella?" Maria asked, in an utterly unsympathetic voice, as if it made me unfit to live in adult society.

I heard the doctor speak from my right side. "There's no record of it, anyway."

And they would know. I felt my face crumple. Yes, they would know very well. They had all my school records, all my records from the various Selecta programs in which I had done everything in my power to avoid anything like this.

I took a deep breath, trying to find some kind of composure. A huge part of me wanted to use this moment, when it seemed like I might be able to persuade the doctor or the guard to go easy on me because, yes, I had never been spanked before—maybe to get them to commute my sentence to a spanking over my panties, over my jeans even. If I said *no* in a pitiful way and cried and begged and apologized for not obeying instantly in the elevator, wouldn't they have mercy?

But the other part of my psyche, the part that had seen me through two sponsors in the Selecta Arrangements program, the part with which I had grown more familiar in the horrid screening exam with Maria... that part rose again, here over the asshole guard's knee.

I took a deep breath and exhaled it hard. I felt my heart rate slowing a little at least. I looked straight at Maria and I said in a voice that impressed me with its hard edge, "No."

Who cares? I don't.

At that moment I became dismayingly aware of an element of this horrendous experience that I had managed until now to push away. As Joe shifted me again on his knee, I felt warm dampness inside my panties, and my cheeks blazed into heat as anger washed through me.

Who cares. I used it: I used the heat of anger that unfortunately seemed to have as company the unwelcome heat of arousal. I relaxed my tense muscles. I looked away from Maria, doing my best to convey the idea that she was beneath my notice.

"There we go," the doctor said, as if something about my response had confirmed a theory. I responded with a grunt of disgust that felt forced and a snort that seemed more natural.

Who cares. For a moment, I felt proud of how I had controlled myself. I didn't give a shit what the doctor had seen or what idea about me it had given him. Then Joe spoke from above me, his voice so patronizing that it made me want to scream.

"Go ahead and take down your jeans and your panties," he said.

Oh no. I froze, with my face turned toward the left—all the way, so that I didn't have to see Maria or, much worse, the mirror. In the glass, I had already seen despite myself a thirty-year-old woman over the knee of a security guard, helpless to avoid a painful, mortifying lesson.

I still had the *who cares* expression on my face; I could feel it in the slackness of my jaw and the raised position of my eyebrows. It had become immobile, though. The rebellious part of me issued an order to my eyes to roll upward so that I could display my indifference, but instead they threatened to close in humiliation as the heat came back into my cheeks.

Why? I demanded of myself desperately. *You knew. They said. Who cares if they see your fucking ass? At least Joe had the decency to let you do it when he had already put you over his knee.*

Despite my best efforts, that thought made my heart race and caused a wince to pass across my face. To my frustration, my eyes did close.

"It's okay, honey," I heard Maria say. "The doctor already knows how aroused you are."

I heard my breath panting through my open lips. *Fuck fuck fuck. How can she just say that shit?*

"I certainly do," said Dr. Hethcote. "No one needs to check your panties, Isabella, to know you're very wet, if that's what you're worried about."

I had no chance at the *who cares* expression, but my mind and my body agreed on something that would at least look stronger than meek pleading or even grateful acceptance of this horrendous scene. I gritted my teeth and I exhaled with a grunt. I didn't protest, either. How fucking weak would it have looked to say, *No, I'm just fucking embarrassed to have this meathead looking at my bare ass. Some of us learned modesty when we were young.*

I clenched my fists, and then with tears I told myself represented rage forming in my eyes, I started to thrust my hands underneath my hips. Joe helpfully shifted his leg and me as I lay across it to make it easier.

Helpfully. Yeah. The gritting of my teeth became grinding as I tried to keep my sobs down. My fingers fumbled at the button on my jeans and got it open. The sudden realization that if I didn't manage to get my panties down inside them Joe and the doctor would *definitely* see a wet spot made my hips jerk with another jolt of humiliating, wanton need.

Hastily, I made sure my thumbs had hooked into the thin stretch cotton.

Wanton curiosity. What was it like, something in me wondered despite everything I tried to shut it the fuck up, to get spanked over a big man's knee? To have to take your panties down so he can teach you to do as you're told?

Well, Isabella, you're about to fucking find out, aren't you?

Angry at myself, angry at the fucks in the room—the asshole security guard, the patronizing nurse, the know-it-all doctor—I found a new way to shove all of that into a corner of my mind. I let the anger take over, and I twisted my face into the deepest scowl I thought my mouth had ever achieved. I pulled my jeans and my panties down to expose my butt.

"Further," Joe said, matter-of-factly. "Middle of your thighs."

The urge to plead with him almost pierced through the hot rage that felt like it had started to choke me. I refused it.

Who cares. Who the fuck cares.

Making sure once again that I had my panties inside them, I complied with Joe's order and drew the jeans down to mid-thigh.

"Far enough?" I demanded, suddenly impressed with my ability to utter such defiant words.

"Isabella," the doctor said, his tone that of someone making an off-hand remark, "you should know that you look extremely unattractive with that expression on your face. Go ahead and give Maria your hands, please, and we can get this over with."

I opened my mouth and closed it, feeling horribly like a fish. I turned as best I could atop the security guard's huge thigh to look at Dr. Hethcote. I had to bring my hands around from under my hips and put them in front of me to keep my balance, such as it was. So just as I caught sight of the doctor's face, his raised eyebrows as he looked back at me the way he might look through a microscope at a virus, I felt Maria take hold first of my right hand, then of my left.

"What the fuck?" I yelled. I felt my body double down on the anger, the rebellion. My limbs, feeling a little stronger after not having resisted for a minute or two, struggled hard. The two horrendous things—the doctor's unbeliev-ably sexist bullshit comment about my expression and the nurse just grabbing my hands—combined to turn me into a white-hot ball of fury.

"Go ahead, Joe," Dr. Hethcote said, as if I were not doing my best impression of a wildcat over the guard's knee. "Isabella, Joe will keep spanking you until you apologize to Maria for disobeying her."

"What... the... fuck!" I screamed the words as I twisted my head toward Maria, then toward the doctor, then even over both shoulders to try to get a look at Joe—maybe to beg for mercy, maybe to see if he was buying into this insanity.

I couldn't turn myself far enough. The huge security guard remained nothing but a set of unyielding muscles— a hand holding me down hard, now, over his knee, another huge leg coming over both of mine to pin them in place with my thighs, I realized to my horror, far enough apart that I knew he could see my shaved pussy.

Another dinner-plate hand, coming down on both my little ass-cheeks with a sharp slap that rang off the walls of the discipline room. I cried out as much in surprise as in pain, but as the second and third spanks fell in the same place, right in the middle of my bottom, I yelled with the burning agony of the lesson Joe seemed intent on delivering.

I would have apologized if you had told me that's what I needed to do. That thought, outlined in blazing red, filled my mind.

EMILY TILTON

Maria gripped my hands harder as I tried to pull them away, desperate to cover my backside. I looked from side to side, looking anywhere but at her or the mirror that showed my utter humiliation.

As Joe's hand rose and fell, I felt like I had been made to ride a seat of fire, there over his knee. I had learned what it felt like to get this kind of lesson, and I didn't like it.

I would have apologized! You didn't have to...

I hated it. I hated them. I cried out in agony.

Or... would I? Would I have said I was sorry?

Tears flowed freely from my eyes. I could literally see the dampness from them on the carpet. I gritted my teeth against my sobs.

I couldn't. I couldn't apologize when it was all such bullshit. A thirty-year-old shouldn't have to obey orders from a nurse, or a doctor, or a security guard. I had signed an agreement, but I hadn't signed away my basic rights, had I?

Had I?

With every spank, my body jerked over the guard's knee. He moved his hand up and down, left and right, so that my whole backside became a blazing torment. I closed my eyes.

"Please," I sobbed, over and over, between the spanks that drew whimpers from deep in my throat. "Please, no."

arl

I watched the video feed from the discipline room from my office three blocks away, in the only skyscraper taller than the Selecta building. In between watching Isabella's screening exam and tuning into her first spanking, I had put the finishing touches on a massive acquisition deal for none other than Selecta itself.

I felt entitled to some self-indulgence. What's more, I knew I had a favor coming from Selecta corporate.

Over the security guard's knee, Isabella had reached that stage of a good, hard, disciplinary spanking where the naughty girl's body just can't take any more. Her data feed, helpfully interpreted by the commentary coming from Selecta's analytic division, showed elevation in every sensory category—pain, arousal, and above all, the emotions that had so clearly begun to overflow in her attempts to hold them back.

Here in Selecta Product Development, they could measure all of that not only with the sensor between her legs but with their amazing suite of biometric algorithms. Hooked up to multiple cameras and enhanced by models based on literally millions of similar young women, those data mining bots—according to the commentary at the bottom of my screen, anyway—said that Isabella Stanford's resistance had broken for the time being.

Don't think her defiance is gone for good! the commentary emphasized as Isabella hung her head and the video switched to a closeup from a camera that must somehow have been installed in the floor. The girl's pretty face had become a mask of woe, the tears flowing freely as her lithe body jerked with each hard spank from the guard's enormous hand.

Expertly, whoever Selecta had put in charge of the video editing switched to a closeup of that punishing hand. The security guard raised it from Isabella's tiny bottom, and before he brought it down again, I could see the sweet, bare pussy of the girl whose progress in this cutting-edge program I had decided I at least must follow.

Selecta had marketed the video feed of the RELM program aggressively to me because just as they could profile their female associate members, helping them match with men who could appreciate—and, if necessary, handle—them, they could, of course, profile those men. They knew I had a certain type, one that lay rather distant from Isabella Stanford's current appearance.

Her responses to dominant stimulation, in the forms both of the nurse's vibrator and the security guard's firm hand, certainly turned me on—I couldn't deny it. I knew myself very well, however, in the romance department—in the fucking department, really. Isabella's body, as pretty as it might be, didn't do it for me.

On the one hand, what a shame—because I had felt an interest in and even a liking for her just from the profile I had seen before tuning into the screening exam. She enjoyed action movies, and she did picture puzzles, and she thought of herself as a suburban homebody despite the urban life Selecta Arrangements girls were more or less forced to live. All of that seemed immensely appealing to me. Isabella had a down-to-earth quality that I had found much too seldom in the girls I'd dated.

What a shame she was tall and flat-chested and narrow-hipped—and from what I had seen so far, not apparently all that submissive. I had no trouble disciplining young women who didn't crave my firm hand, certainly, but unless a girl had a genuine submissive side, the relationship wouldn't go anywhere after that. Despite what Selecta seemed to think about Isabella, she currently didn't seem like the kind of woman who could end up next to me at the altar with the understanding that she would, as old-fashioned as it sounded, honor and obey me

—and take regular trips across my knee when she forgot her duties in one way or another.

But Selecta had presented me with the opportunity to watch this bright, pretty, still at thirty very young woman undergo the RELM program for a reason. Would the program fulfill its promise?

Isabella gave a final sob and raised her eyes to look the nurse in the eyes.

* * *

Isabella

"I'm sorry," I choked out.

I tried to forget about the mirror behind Maria. Really, it should have been easy, I could simply focus on her face—on her eyes, which had become a great deal more sympathetic and a great deal less patronizing. As she nodded to acknowledge my apology, I thought I could even tell that the nurse really did feel compassion for the distress I had gotten myself into.

"Thank you, Isabella," she said. "I know you'll do better, going forward."

I could have kept my attention on Maria's face, or I could have closed my eyes, but her words made me think about the way I had just learned a difficult lesson, the way a little girl, or even—in some small towns—a girl not yet twenty, learns obedience. My eyes found their way to the side of Maria's blue scrub-clad hip, to my own face in the mirror. I saw my pout of helpless submission to the firm hand of the massive guard who loomed above me in the old-fashioned wooden chair.

I felt the heat from that hand, which Joe had rested on my ass, fingers squeezing gently as if to comfort me. I couldn't see it. I couldn't see the hand or my backside, which I knew had to have taken on the color of a flaming sunset.

The guard who had punished me could see my bottom— and the horrible doctor could see it.

Girls who don't know how to behave don't get to have a say about their bottoms. I swallowed hard at the barely rational but distressingly arousing thought.

To my horror, between my legs, the heat from my bottom and my upper thighs, enhanced by the slight movement of Joe's huge, strong fingers, seemed to rush into my pussy. Only half intending the movement, I started to struggle against the guard's right leg, still clamped down over both of mine. I needed to close my thighs, or I might leave a wet spot on Joe's pants.

My face went hot, and I saw the blush in the mirror, and I finally did close my eyes because I just couldn't bear to keep looking at the naughty girl over the big man's knee.

"You can go ahead and let her up, Joe," Dr. Hethcote said. "Isabella, you may pull up your pants."

Oh God. The very idea of needing permission—the way it implied how the doctor would treat me here in Selecta Product Development—made my heart race with panic.

Then he made it much worse.

"I can see how aroused it got you to be punished with your panties down," he said. "That's natural for a young woman like you. Nothing to worry about."

Maria let go of my hands, and I scrambled to pull up my jeans and panties, doing everything I could to keep my pussy hidden as I did. I wondered wildly for a moment whether Joe would have something to say about my arousal, and an insane part of me even seemed to *want* him to say something... though I had no idea what he could say that wouldn't make me literally disintegrate into a fine mist of sheer embarrassment.

He stayed silent, though, as he helped me onto my feet. I kept my eyes down on the carpet, trying to will the heat in my face away. The doctor's words echoed in my head: *a young woman like you.*

For what felt like the first time, I realized that since this ordeal had begun with Maria's visit to my apartment this morning, I had heard that a lot. Both the nurse and the doctor clearly had some idea that I belonged in a special category—and that being in that category meant I...

Meant I... what?

I tried to bite back my words, but they came out before I could stop them. I raised my eyes to Dr. Hethcote and demanded, "What does that mean? *A young woman like you?*"

He glanced over at Maria. I followed his gaze and saw that she had raised her eyebrows in response. I did manage to turn my snort of anger at their patronizing attitude into a simple exhalation. They clearly thought me a very interesting specimen. Fuck them and their megacorp.

"Joe," the doctor said, "you can go. Thanks for your help."

I looked at the hard-muscled guard, who had turned to me. "No hard feelings, Isabella?" he asked.

My eyes went very wide, and then my brows knit. "N-no," I stammered. What else could I say?

"Thanks," he said. "I know you're going to be a good girl from now on."

My lips parted and my breathing sped up. *That. That's what I wanted him to say.* As the heat surged back into my face, I looked down at the carpet again.

"My pleasure, doctor," he said, and started toward the door.

I raised my eyes so that I could watch the doctor as he followed Joe's progress out the door of the discipline room. I got the strong impression that he was waiting to tell me something private or maybe even secret. I supposed I should be grateful because I had the even stronger impression that what Dr. Hethcote would tell me would humiliate me yet again.

The heavy door closed behind Joe's broad back. The doctor turned to me.

"Isabella, do you think of yourself as submissive?" he asked.

I felt my face twist into a look of bewilderment. My brows knitted and my mouth tightened, even as I felt a hot surge of blood in my neck. I looked over at Maria, hoping to see on the nurse's face that she had the same opinion I did of this utterly inappropriate question.

Even as I turned my eyes to her, though, I remembered the much worse things she had said while she had used the horrible toy between my legs. I couldn't remember— had she used the word *submissive*? Why did it matter? The young wife she had depicted as she brought me to my humiliating first orgasm, that busty, curvy girl who needed her husband's firm hand, couldn't be described any other way, could she?

I rearranged my features into a cold sneer, taking advantage of the mirror to help me pull my mouth over exactly as far as made me look as uninterested as possible in Dr. Hethcote's question. I met his eyes again.

"What's that supposed to mean?" I replied, as if the answer could never have even the most trivial connection to me.

I had a sudden urge, nevertheless, to put my hands behind me, to shield my backside from more of their crazy "discipline"—and, I realized with an unwelcome jolt between my thighs, to rub my ass-cheeks and ease the sting that pulling up my jeans had caused there. The lingering effects of Joe's big hand added a distracting element to this awful conversation with the doctor.

My hands stayed resolutely at my hips, where I tightened them into fists. I watched the doctor glance down at his tablet with that horrid little look that seemed to tell him everything he needed to know about me, based solely on the device the nurse had put between my legs. He nodded slightly and looked up at me.

"You may go ahead and rub your bottom, if you like," he said, as if the words represented an answer to my question—and as if I had, in his degrading product development program, lost the right to touch my own body without permission.

My lips parted, though I had nothing to say in words. The anger and fear that rose in my chest wanted to come out in some scream of defiance, but instead my breathing just sped up,

Tears welled in the corners of my eyes, which I could see in the mirror were already red from crying over Joe's knee as he had punished me. I closed my mouth and gritted my teeth.

"No, thank you," I said with as much scorn as I could muster.

"Suit yourself," said the doctor. "The answer to your question, Isabella, about what it means to be a girl like you, is a sizable part of why you're here. Another part is that you don't know what kind of girl you are, and this program will, among other things, help you learn."

I blinked at him, frowning. He turned to Maria.

"Let's get her settled. We'll start her treatment in half an hour."

CHAPTER 8

 *sabella*

Maria escorted me to a little bedroom. It didn't look like a hospital room or even the generic sort of room I had expected when she opened the door. My wide eyes beheld a space that my brain, pulling from somewhere I couldn't identify, some old movie or something, instantly called a *boudoir*.

Pink. Lots of pink. Not my favorite color, at least since I had turned eighteen. I liked light blues, shading into teal.

The same part of my brain that had supplied the word *boudoir* asked me a question then, a seemingly innocent one that my *who cares* mindset rejected with contempt.

Why are you wearing pink panties then?

I *had* blue panties—and black ones, and beige ones. I had some of them in the bag I saw someone had put on a pink and white luggage rack in one corner of this bedroom. But, yes, I had chosen to put on pink ones this morning.

Who cares?

I looked at the pink and cream vanity, with its triple mirror, and the silver-backed hairbrush and comb resting atop it. I looked at the old-fashioned floral-painted dresser, and at the queen-sized bed with its striped, pink coverlet. My cheeks, I knew, had turned a shade to match the decor.

"As I'm sure you've guessed," Maria told me, "the researchers have surveillance in this room, but they turn it off between nine at night and seven in the morning to give you privacy."

I noticed then that two doors led from the room, which seemed odd for a little bedroom like this one.

"Two closets?" I asked, frowning.

"No," the nurse replied, walking over to the door nearest to her and opening it. "You've got a connecting bathroom, for… convenience."

My frown deepened as I heard the strange pause Maria had put before she had said *convenience*. As I stepped toward the door she had just opened to take a look at the facilities, I wondered if she had almost said something else—and exactly whose convenience we were talking about.

The bathroom seemed almost as big as the bedroom. It had a bidet—I barely knew the name of the strange thing next to the toilet, let alone how to use it. It had a separate shower big enough for at least two people. It had a huge jacuzzi tub.

All in coral pink.

My jaw dropped and, of course, my blush deepened.

I needed something to say, and I needed it fast. I needed to say it in the *who cares* voice. For a moment I chewed the inside of my cheek, and then I found the perfect response.

"They're watching in here too, right?"

I felt a little thrill of pride in the scornful sound in my voice, even as my mind raced, trying to figure out the bathroom. What did it mean? What did the vanity mean, and the hairbrush, and the dresser?

A thrill of angry shame shot through me as I remembered the doctor's question. *Isabella, do you think of yourself as submissive?*

No. Absolutely not.

But... what the fuck did a frilly pink bedroom and a huge pink bathroom have to do with being submissive? Was it just a mind fuck, none of it having anything to do with anything else? Like the idea was to drop me into an utterly surreal environment and watch me fall apart, then see if they could market whatever remained as a new "product"?

I felt myself bite my lip, as if I were observing another person's body, and then I realized that had happened because my right hand had drifted back behind me. To my horror, I had started to rub my sore bottom. Just a little, but... I bit my lip harder because I knew beyond any doubt that it would show up on the horrible sensor between my legs.

They clearly thought me intelligent. I had always scored well on IQ tests and aptitude measurements, despite my failure to "go" anywhere in life so far. So, a voice in my head said I needed to stop pretending I didn't understand: my body clearly had made a connection my mind didn't want to acknowledge.

My blush got hotter. I couldn't give in, no matter what they saw in the "data" coming from between my thighs. Angrily, I pulled my hand from the seat of my jeans.

"Of course," Maria replied. "But again, not between nine and seven."

I nodded, trying as hard as I could to set my face into a grim mask of resentment.

Maria closed the bathroom door. "I'll let you settle in a little. Your treatments will happen just down the hall, and I'll come get you when it's time. You'll have lunch right after that, and then you're free to use the fitness center or the lounge, or to stay here in your room. There's a workstation on the vanity to get online if you want."

The sheer normality of these words calmed my nerves and let the blood recede from my face and, even better, from the troublesome lower regions where the stupid bathroom had, for some reason, brought the unexpected, unwelcome heat.

"Okay," I said, nodding. "Sounds like a vacation."

Maria smiled. "Yes. Think of it that way, and I think you're going to have a good stay here."

My mouth twitched briefly to the side. "You can't tell me anything more about the treatments?" I asked, hoping to take advantage of what seemed like a moment of sympathy between us.

Maria shook her head. "That's an important part of the protocol," she said. "But there's one thing you should remember, even though I know it seems like they say it so much it can't be true."

I felt my brows knit. "I can trust Selecta?" I guessed.

Maria nodded. "It's really not because they're, you know, good people or anything. It's because making people happy and healthy is just good business—and keeping the economy running depends on it."

"If you say so," I said, trying to make the words more ironic than sarcastic.

Maria laughed. "I think you'll see, even if the journey is sometimes a little…"

She glanced down, toward my jeans. A flash of heat blazed in my cheeks.

"… uncomfortable," she finished.

* * *

Twenty minutes later, Maria knocked on my door.

"You'll need to take off your clothes," she told me matter-of-factly.

Despite her having given me exactly the same command back at my apartment, it still took me by surprise this time. I stared at her.

"The facility is kept warm enough that you won't be cold," she said.

"But..." My face reddened as my mind sought some way out. By this time I didn't think I had misunderstood, because so much else of the "program" had already proven itself humiliating and bizarre. "But... in the hallway? Couldn't I take them off... you know, when I..."

My voice trailed off as I saw the look on Maria's face—the firm one I had encountered so many times there already. The one that said that in her job she had seen hundreds of young women try to get out of the requirements they had imposed on themselves, really. I had signed the agreement, and clearly the agreement said that if Selecta wanted me naked in the hallway of the product development facility, I would obey.

Or... I blew a snort of air through my nose, trying to dispel the heat that had just surged to my cheeks. *Dammit.* Much as I had tried simply to forget my degrading trip across the security guard's knee, the memory had remained lodged in the front of my mind.

Joe's huge hand falling over and over, spanking my thirty-year-old bottom, bare as a little girl's who had stolen a piece of candy from the corner store. Me, writhing, sobbing, and finally relaxing into my terrible lesson. Joe, squeezing me there gently as if to tell me I had become a good girl again, having submitted to his discipline.

Submitted.

Fuck.

I swallowed hard as I waited for Maria to deny the request that seemed utterly reasonable to me.

Who cares.

I didn't let her answer. "Whatever," I said, and turned around so I wouldn't have to watch her watching me undress. As I pulled my shirt over my head, she did respond, though. Her words made me wish I hadn't even tried.

"You should think about why you do care about it, Isabella," she said. "We're all medical professionals here. We know what a young woman's body looks like. Think about why you care and why we have the rule that you must be naked when you go for your treatment."

I ripped the shirt off, over my head—practically tearing the fabric, so I could turn to look at the nurse. I swiveled only my head, and I held the tee over my breasts, and I knew my cheeks had gone crimson.

I didn't know why, though. Yes, modesty—but wasn't Maria right? Why should I care? And yet I wouldn't be telling myself over and over *not* to care if I didn't, would I?

The nurse's face looked back at me impassively. I almost pleaded with her yet again to tell me more about the program. Her words had had the effect she had certainly intended. My thoughts and feelings had become a confused jumble as I considered the two questions—why did I care, and why did Selecta care—and what connection lay between them and whatever actual treatment I was about to receive?

Did they just want to scare me out of my mind? No, because they could have done that much more effectively with, like, creepy metal instruments or something.

They probably did want to scare me… but not too much? And… maybe… in a certain way?

My heart rate had sped up as my mind flashed through all these questions. A surge of anger—at Maria, at Selecta, at myself—flared in my chest, and I tried to use it to push all my stupid thoughts about modesty away. I turned back toward the vanity, refusing to look at the mirrors there, and I dropped the t-shirt atop it. I reached for the button of my jeans.

Who cares. Fine, the horrible nurse had alarmed me with the idea that *I* cared no matter how much I told myself I didn't. But the phrase represented my most important defense, and I stuck with it. *Who cares? Not me.*

I unbuttoned my jeans and pulled them down, with my— yes, fine—pink panties inside.

Naked, I followed Maria down the hall. She hadn't lied about the temperature. The medical professionals wearing clothes must have felt quite warm, because it felt like a day at the beach in the underground facility. It was well insulated, I was sure, but in this day and age of rolling blackouts—and in some regions of the country, just unending blackouts—the necessary energy must represent an extravagance.

A tax write-off, probably, my brain said, trying to push away my consciousness of walking nude down a perfectly respectable corridor. Did Selecta even pay taxes?

The treatment room lay only twenty steps away and a sign outside the open door said *TREATMENT*. Inside, the room was small, its space dominated by what looked like a phone booth from an old movie, though much sleeker— and with a metal device hanging down from its ceiling, visible through its transparent window-walls.

A lab tech sat at the counter in the corner of the room: a woman of about Maria's age—forty or so, in scrubs. There was a simple plastic chair near the counter, and I saw on top of the counter near the chair a little disposable plastic cup, close enough for me to make out a single white pill at its bottom. Next to the cup was another one, with what was probably water in it, though here in Selecta's dungeon, who knew.

"You can go ahead and sit down, Isabella," the tech said in a bored-sounding voice. "I'll let the doctor know you're here."

I looked at Maria, succeeding, I thought, in keeping my anxiety off my face. She nodded.

"I'll come get you when the treatment is over and take you to lunch," she told me. She must have seen a trace of panic in my eyes because she said, "We'll go back to your room first, so you can get dressed."

She left the room, and I went to sit in the chair, which felt very strange against my naked backside. The surface was hard too, and to my dismay I squirmed involuntarily as I felt the soreness Joe's firm hand had left behind. I scowled as a twinge between my thighs came along with the squirm.

Then I raised my eyes to the tech to see if she had noticed, and I found her looking back at me with an expression that made me think she had tried, mostly successfully, to hide a smile.

Fuck. Fuck you. I looked back at her defiantly.

"Go ahead and take the pill," she said. "Dr. Hethcote will be here in a moment."

sabella

I gazed down at the ordinary-looking pill in the plastic cup. I felt absolutely certain that the tech wouldn't tell me what the medicine was if I had asked. Maybe she didn't even know.

You can trust Selecta.

I knew I could trust them to do their best to turn me into something marketable. I took the pill.

A knock sounded at the door, and the doctor came in, the way doctors do, without waiting for anyone to invite them in. Like they own the place.

Like he owned me, his research subject.

I couldn't help it, I put my hands up to cover myself, and hunched down in the chair. I felt my face melt into a frightened look as the doctor strode in, but I changed it into a dismissive sneer, though I didn't succeed in relaxing my body.

I didn't take my hands away from my chest and my lap either, because that would have looked stupid and weak. Also, the asshole doctor should understand that even if modesty had become an outdated notion, a young woman deserved a little *privacy*, anyway.

To my dismay, Dr. Hethcote raised his eyebrows with a little smile, as if my attempt to keep him from seeing my unfortunately extremely hard nipples amused him no end.

"Hi again, Isabella," he said. "Why don't you stand up for me and head into the treatment booth?"

He crossed the short distance to the thing on the other side of the room and pulled the door open.

I looked at him for a long moment, taking deep breaths through my nose, willing him to say something more. The doctor just looked back at me, the same little smile on his face.

The technician, still seated at the counter, said, as if I had insulted her by not rising eagerly and getting into her bizarre contraption, "It's perfectly safe, Isabella."

I looked over at her. I swallowed hard, still putting so much effort into keeping my face from crumpling that I could hardly think of anything else.

"But what *is* it?" I asked, my voice falling to a whisper as if maybe the doctor couldn't hear me and the tech would impart the knowledge for which I was so desperate as a special, secret favor.

"It does two things, actually," the doctor replied.

I looked back at him, a little surprised that he had answered my question at all, based on his previous refusal to tell me anything worth hearing. "It activates the medication you just took and it scans your body to give us a sense of what that medication is doing."

Oh. He had answered because he had no intention of actually answering.

I knew I should stop myself and should either get into the fucking booth or try—absolutely futilely, I felt certain—to escape from the agreement I had so stupidly made. Instead, I asked the question I knew he wouldn't answer.

"The medication... it... I mean, when it's activated... what...?"

I didn't even really ask. I just made myself look foolish. The doctor nodded, though, as if I had said something intelligent—but also as if I had said something intelligent not for a thirty-year-old but for a dog or a horse.

"I understand how frustrating this is, Isabella," he said, "but I'm afraid the treatment—and thus the research you're participating in, as well—depends on you not knowing any more at this point. One thing I can tell you is that you'll be an active participant in the treatment, starting right now. You're going to tell us how you're feeling to the best of your ability, and we're going to adjust your therapy to match your experience."

My jaw slackened. This was actually a bunch of new information—but the kind of information that makes you realize just how much you don't know. I stared at the doctor, trying to process everything he had said.

He nodded again and gave a little sigh as he glanced down at his tablet. Then he looked up at me again.

"All I can tell you, Isabella, is that the goal of this research is to make girls like you happy—as well as your sponsors. If you want to opt out of the treatment now, you can. You'll lose the money, obviously, but the choice is yours. I won't even have you spanked again. We'll just send you home."

I squirmed on the seat, furious at myself for the jolt of need that had accompanied the reference to the horrible little scene in the discipline room.

Who cares? Not me. I needed the fucking money, and… I wanted a sponsor.

I stood up, putting my hands at my side and managing not to flinch or to look too awkward as I revealed my tiny breasts and the hint of the shaved cleft between my thighs. I walked over to the booth.

"Good girl," the doctor said.

Ugh. Asshole.

I stepped into the booth. At least the transparent walls made it feel more space-aged than claustrophobic. The doctor closed the glass door with a click, and then the machinery above me and—I sensed—around me, whirred into life.

The tech spoke from across the room, and I realized I could hear her voice on a speaker inside the booth.

"Turn to face the doctor, Isabella, please. There are handles to either side of you. You can go ahead and take hold of them."

I obeyed, looking for the handles and finding them protruding from the glass of the walls, made of the same material. I began to get the feeling the material, transparent and hard, glasslike in every respect, must be something else, something full of strange energy. I swallowed hard as my fingers closed around the smooth surface.

I raised my eyes to look through the door out at the little treatment room and at Dr. Hethcote and the tech sitting there. I felt the heat rise in my cheeks as I became conscious again of my nakedness. They hadn't restrained me in any way but somehow, having to hold the handles *felt* like a kind of... the word floated into my brain and I couldn't stop it... bondage.

The doctor glanced down at his tablet.

Asshole. My brow had threatened to furrow in embarrassment—at my vulnerability, my nudity, and above all at the stupid way it affected me down there. Instead, I put the *who cares* scowl on my face.

The doctor kept his eyes on the screen, and I realized he must be studying my sensor data. That thought made me even angrier.

He nodded and spoke.

"Now," he said.

I felt my eyes widen as I looked over at the technician and saw that she had a tablet of her own and had begun to slide her finger along it. I tightened my grip on the handles, expecting... something.

Above me, maybe two feet away, I heard three clicks, and then a beep. I looked at the doctor, who had raised his gaze to me again. Seconds went by.

"Is something...?" I asked, remembering what he had said just before I had gotten into the booth about my participation.

Then the voice—not the doctor's or the tech's but someone else's, so vivid it sounded as if the speaker was in the booth with me—started to talk to me. A man with a pleasant baritone said, "You've always wanted big tits, haven't you, Isabella? Real cleavage... melons that would fill out the kind of dress a slip of a girl like you can never wear."

The voice itself, as much as the degrading words, caused my body's reaction. It seemed to envelop me in the booth, inviting me to close my eyes and picture the terrible image the unseen man had introduced into my mind. He spoke soothingly, and yet he used phrases that sent shock-waves of humiliation through my entire nervous system with every syllable.

Big tits. Melons. Oh no. And… *slip of a girl.*

Somehow, they knew what had lain inside me ever since my eighteenth birthday and my realization that I would never grow the kind of breasts that I thought meant *you are a woman.*

My whole body bucked: my hips led the way, mortifyingly, my knees bending, my chest thrusting itself out and my face puckering into an expression I knew would tell the doctor much too much about what the voice had done to me.

The defiant, who-cares indifference remained there, somewhere in my mind. So I tried to resist the apparently ever-new impulse to cover myself again that took hold of me. Without success—my hands attempted with all their might to rise up off the handles and throw themselves over my chest and my lap. Every fiber of my being wanted somehow to hide my shameful physical response to the filthy words the unknown man had said, and the ones he now proceeded to say.

"And your ass, Isabella…"

It felt to me as if I heard the word *ass* at the same moment I realized my hands had become stuck to the handles—that something in my muscles or my nerves or both simply couldn't let go. My eyes flew open and I saw Dr.

Hethcote looking back at me intently. A slight frown seemed to indicate that he cared about my distress, and to my dismay I took a little comfort from that.

He cares about you as a product, said a nasty voice in my mind. *He cares about... about your* ass *as a product.*

It all unfolded inside my head in an instant, and it brought a sob from my chest even as the voice continued.

"You've always wanted a nice, big, heart-shaped bottom, haven't you?"

No. No, please.

"The kind of backside a wealthy husband loves to see as his wife walks away at a party, maybe, dressed in a slinky black dress. He turns to a friend and sees the friend watching you too, in your heels, the tight silky fabric molding your perfect ass. He knows his friend is thinking about what's going to happen later that night in your bedroom, with the lights on the way your husband likes it."

I had closed my eyes again, because the part of me that wanted to see the impossible, unbearably sexy vision had simply overwhelmed the part that tried to keep it out.

"Say *yes*, Isabella," said the voice. "That's all. Say yes to the big boobs, the curves, the sweet ass."

Oh no. The picture, the video playing inside my head glowed, it seemed to me. The party and then the bedroom. The lights on, so he could see me as he undressed me, first to the sexy black lingerie he had told me to wear to the party—a bustier with a corset, my waist small between the curves of my enormous breasts and my flared hips... tiny black panties... sheer thigh-high stockings.

The lingerie still on me, the panties merely pulled aside so my husband could fuck me, bent over the bed, his cock flashing, his lap pounding against my rounded bottom-cheeks.

In the booth, I felt my hips buck. In my mind, I came and came with his hardness inside me. Here in the real world, though, my tingling clit, my aching vagina, made me feel so needy that all thought of feigned indifference flew out the window.

"Yes," I sobbed.

"Good girl," said the voice, and then I heard a beep, and three more clicks. I still felt the arousal in my stiff nipples as the air from the booth's ventilation moved over them, and in my pussy, as my knees bounced with the after-shocks of the fantasy. Their intensity had subsided, though, in some way I couldn't define.

I found I could move my hands again, and to my disgust they instantly flew back to my chest and my pussy. My jaw slackened as my fingers touched the places that should feel so familiar.

Did I feel *different* there? Was I going crazy, or did my breasts feel just a little rounder, and my thighs feel a tiny bit fuller?

Trying to sound more angry than desperate, I peered out at the doctor.

"What the fuck was *that*?" I demanded.

arl

Selecta took an audio sample of my voice when they registered me for access to RELM. The one that had come out of the speakers in Isabella's treatment booth hadn't actually sounded exactly like mine—my voice was a lot deeper, for one—but the cadence and intonation had matched mine very closely, just as Selecta's marketing materials had said they would.

Once you've put a down payment on a RELM girl's contract, their email offering me a special low buy-in rate had advised, *her treatment will contain subtle yet crucially important elements related to you, her intended sponsor. This shaping of the changes she will undergo won't make her your willing servant, of course, or even guarantee that she'll accept the contract, but it certainly sets the stage beautifully for a very special relationship. And if she doesn't accept your sponsorship in the end, Selecta will refund your down payment—or you can roll it over to another RELM girl or a different Selecta offering such as a platinum New Modesty account.*

I studied Isabella's face as she looked at herself in the mirror back in her room. They hadn't answered her question, of course, as to the nature of her treatment. Her mystification represented an important part of the therapy—nor would Isabella have understood if they had tried to explain.

She would have grasped the basic idea, certainly, just as I did. I didn't understand it, though, in any more than the most superficial way.

Apparently—and the slight but definitely noticeable changes in her body demonstrated that Selecta's outlandish claims were true at some level at least—Dr. Hethcote had built the RELM on Selecta's pioneering research into the ability of the mind to shape the body. Specifically, the ability of the libidinal areas of the limbic system to cause cells to express their DNA in radically different ways than they had hitherto done.

Any high school biology course these days spent time talking about how much information DNA contains, and how little of it actually gets expressed, at least in ways that we understand. It seemed that Selecta had found parts of it that controlled certain key physiological features. More importantly, they had also discovered ways to shape those features, through DNA expression: the top-secret medication—which might have been a sugar pill for all I could understand about the process, the high-frequency electro-magnetic stimulation from above and, crucially, in the wave that seemed to run from one of Isabella's hands to the other in the booth's handles.

And what I couldn't help but think of as the *secret sauce*. The voice, saying filthy things, stirring forbidden desires. Helping a girl accept her submissive needs even as those needs and the fantasies they evoked literally reshaped her body.

Isabella frowned at herself in the mirror and began to chew the inside of her cheek. She had her left arm across her bare tummy in a sort of idle protective gesture, while her right hand went from one of her now practically B cup breasts to the other.

My own heart rate sped up as I looked at her, thinking about the parts of her treatment Selecta had invited me to contribute to. One of them would take a few more days to show up, but I wondered whether another had started to become visible already—and whether part of the pensive look on Isabella's face resulted from her noticing it.

I started to get hard as I watched from my office, and Isabella hadn't even noticed my third contribution to her treatment which lay on the bed, lacy and cream-colored, awaiting her with a note from me.

* * *

Isabella

.   .   .

I realized that they had taken away my luggage before I saw the nightgown on the bed. At first, when I saw that my purple bag had disappeared, along with the luggage stand on which it had rested, I thought someone must have put it in the closet. When I opened the closet, though, I saw no bag and no luggage stand, but instead someone else's clothes—lots of pink, lots of sequins and beads.

Confused but still thinking mostly about the utterly weird changes from the treatment—and the even stranger way they made me feel—I went to the dresser. Maybe someone had actually unpacked my clothes and put them away. In the top drawer I found someone else's under-wear—presumably, the same woman whose dresses hung in the closet.

Some of the bras and panties were pink, others were white and cream, still others red or black. There were a few sets of normal-looking things—as it seemed to me anyway: little-girl type cotton and more adult beige and black. But the laciness and satin sheen of the more complicated things sent a wave of heat to my cheeks.

Then I saw the black bustier with its lace-up corset, off to the side of that drawer. I frowned deeply, suddenly much more conscious of my nakedness.

That was in my head, I thought desperately. *The voice didn't say anything about a corset. These aren't mine. They aren't.*

I hadn't brought my *who cares* face back after the treatment. Thankfully, I hadn't really needed to. Though Dr.

Hethcote hadn't answered my questions, Maria had arrived right after the end of the session in the booth and led me away. By the time I had stepped out of the booth, I had seemed to forget my anger at the doctor.

I had felt... bemused. I had felt, well... *good*. I had reached my room and entered it. Maria had closed the door behind me with the instruction to get dressed and the information that she would return in twenty minutes to take me to lunch. I had gone to the full-length mirror on the back of the closet door and stood there, touching my chest vaguely, trying to figure out whether I had imagined the change I had felt in the booth, in the wake of the dirty, degrading things the voice had said to me and the even more mortifying fantasy they had inspired.

Part of me had thought—had *known*—I should feel angry and humiliated. Somehow, I simply didn't have access to those emotions. I couldn't muster the *who cares* attitude with which I had responded to them, either. It had served as an adequate defense mechanism against the stupid situation in which I had gotten myself—into which Selecta had *put* me, something in my brain corrected.

Looking at myself in the mirror, I grew more and more certain that my breasts *had* gotten bigger and—even more embarrassingly, but also strangely gratifyingly—my backside *had* grown a little rounder. It had made the situation seem less stupid and my role more important. Maybe I had made a good decision after all, to join this program despite the indignity involved?

I had no idea how it could be possible—everything I knew about human physiology said that you couldn't gain that much tissue in the ten minutes the treatment had lasted. But then, I didn't actually know very much about human physiology or about what technology Selecta might have developed since my biology textbook had been written.

My breasts were bigger. I looked down at the bras in the top drawer of the dresser. They couldn't be mine—they were C cups. I might be a B cup now, after the treatment, assuming I hadn't gone insane and Dr. Hethcote hadn't actually altered my brain chemistry somehow so that I had entered some fantasy world.

I looked at the panties, a large. I wore a small, and I didn't think my ass had enlarged enough for medium. Pulling out one of the lacy red thongs, I felt another surge of heat to my cheeks. The man in my fantasy—not the one whose voice it was, but the one he had seemed to talk about—my husband... he would want to make me get into these, before he...

I swallowed hard and dropped the other girl's panties. I closed the drawer and turned around, wondering what the hell Maria had meant me to get dressed in. Did she not know that someone had come in and apparently moved me out of this room? Where was the woman whose clothes now occupied the closet and the dresser?

Then I saw the nightgown on the bed and the note lying on top of it.

A pink babydoll nightgown. Very lacy. A *bow* on the front. Too big for me on top, instinct told me. The kind of thing that wouldn't look good on me, I knew, since I didn't have the curves for it.

A *bow* on the front. My eyes kept going back to it, maybe so that I didn't have to think about the note. Like... the girl wearing it was a...

A present.

The note—notes went with presents. The doctor? No, I could see the name at the top of the notecard—Carl Thring.

A man, the kind of man who had engraved notecards... giving me a lacy pink nightgown as a present?

The kind of man who gives expensive lingerie as a present.

I felt a tremor in my knees as I was finally forced to an understanding about the clothes in the closet and the dresser.

Mine. My new clothes.

My brow furrowed hard. The stuff in the closet... definitely not my taste.

I picked up the note. My jaw dropped as I began to read it.

Dear Isabella, let me introduce myself with this first gift. My name is Carl Thring. I'm an executive who works here in Chicago. I don't work for Selecta, though my firm does business with them. That connection gave me the opportunity to become acquainted with you and your involvement in your current treatment program, and I've accepted Selecta's offer to become your prospective sponsor.

My heart thudded in my chest. I looked down at the nightgown, at the bow. A man I had never met... he had *become acquainted* with me, and...

He wants me. The words sounded primal in my mind, but the note seemed to have stirred primal feelings.

I bit my lip and kept reading, utterly unable to name the mixture of emotions that seemed to boil in my chest.

Once we meet, you'll have the chance to say no, of course, but being your prospective sponsor gives me the opportunity to help guide your treatment.

My eyes went wide. "What?" I said aloud, and now I couldn't stop reading, though part of me felt like tearing the heavy notecard up and burning the pieces.

I've decided you're going to be the kind of girl who wears this nightgown every night while you wait for a man like me to come home and fuck you.

"Oh my God," I whispered. From painstakingly polite to lewd and crude in a single sentence. My breath had gotten ragged between my parted lips.

That's all I can tell you now, after your first treatment—except to add that you're to put this nightgown on and wear it for the rest of the day.

I'm looking forward very much indeed to meeting you, Isabella.

Yours,

Carl

I dropped the note onto the pink comforter, next to the pink nightgown.

Mine? I laughed weakly at the irony. Hadn't he just told me, more or less, that I was *his*—that Selecta had given, or more likely sold, me to him?

But... he *must* be a luxury sponsor, right? Beyond that, maybe... he had to be immensely wealthy to have that level of access.

I reached down to the bed, to finger the delicate silk of the nightgown. So soft and smooth. Too big on top, yes, but not as much as it would have been an hour ago. The blush surged back into my face as more pieces of the bizarre program I had enrolled in fell into place.

Looking down, with my right hand on the silky fabric, I found my left hand had gone to my breasts, to my nipples. A feeling of heaviness there—something I had never, ever experienced before—sent a wave of tingling arousal through me, stiffening the little bud under my finger.

Before I could even think about it, that hand moved down over my flat tummy to find the cleft between my legs.

I gasped as I touched my clit with two fingertips, the lightest pressure sending a wave of need into my thighs and hips. Into my bottom-cheeks, where I realized the pain of the spanking had vanished entirely.

But Carl... he would...

My fingers worked their way down. I gazed at the bow that would make the girl wearing the nightgown into a gift, a present for her master.

Would he? Would he spank me, if…

I swallowed hard as I found out just how much wetness lay just inside my aching sheath.

I had never, ever done this, but something seemed so… different now. I thrust two fingers inside my vagina and gathered the juices. I spread them up, forward. My right hand went back, behind me, and took hold of my bottom-cheek, feeling how it had gotten bigger.

I cried out, my eyes closing, thinking of Carl Thring, wondering what he looked like.

The door opened, and Maria said, "Stop that, Isabella. Right now."

CHAPTER 11

 sabella

I gasped and turned around, my hands moving to cover my naked breasts and pussy yet again. The nurse's expression seemed, for just a moment, to have some sympathy in it—a softness around the eyes, maybe, as if she thought she could understand what it felt like to have your whole idea about yourself transformed, and even to have your body changed to match.

That hint of condescension, though, helped me find my resistance. My own face had started out in the mortifying pout it had worn as I looked down at the nightgown and couldn't keep from touching myself as I thought about the horrible, degrading note from Carl Thring.

Horrid. Degrading. Yes.

Heat blazed in my cheeks as I forced those words into the front of my mind, and the look on Maria's face drove the arousal from me. I straightened up, realizing only as I did so that my upper body had bent a little, pushing my backside out, in a mortifying involuntary movement—as if I had meant to present my bottom to my sponsor's firm hand.

That pushed my attitude all the way over the edge. I tossed my head as I put the sneer back on my lips. I lowered my hands as if I didn't give a shit whether Maria looked at my strangely growing breasts and my slightly broader lap.

"So I'm not allowed to touch my own body now?" I asked, but not in any urgent tone. I spoke as if I didn't care in the slightest.

"No," the nurse confirmed. "Not that way—not without permission."

My jaw dropped and the blush, which I had managed to drive away with the *who cares* expression, surged into my cheeks again. With difficulty, I recovered the sarcastic curl of my lips.

"Any chance you'll tell me why?" Again, blasé, as if the answer didn't matter to me at all, though a voice at the back of my mind—a voice I didn't think I had ever heard before—had started to wail in protest and frustration.

"Sure," she responded. "Your sexual arousal drives the physiological process that's started inside you. Orgasm has a big part to play in that, and you'll only be allowed to have one when your therapy dictates. The same goes for masturbation that doesn't lead to orgasm, in case you're wondering, what's usually called edging. When the time comes, you won't just be given permission—you'll be required to do both."

It took everything in my power to keep my breathing even and my eyes from opening much wider than would have gone with my defiant expression. I knew she expected me to ask *When is that?* I could see it on her face. I refused. Instead, I cast a scornful glance down at the nightgown on the bed.

"You want me to put this on, right?" I asked. "That's why you left it out for me."

"Yes, Isabella," she said, her eyes turning maddeningly sympathetic once again. "Go ahead and put on the nightgown, and we'll go to lunch."

I ate alone in a little dining area just down the hall from my room: sausage soup, a huge roast beef sandwich with chips, and to my surprise, a big piece of yellow cake with chocolate buttercream frosting. Maria wheeled it all in on a cart.

"Really?" I asked when I saw the cake.

"Really," she said. "Your body needs a lot of calories right now."

I did. I wolfed down the soup, the sandwich, and the chips —I hadn't even realized how hungry I had gotten. I took my time with the cake, though. I hadn't allowed myself dessert in a long, long time.

To my dismay, it made me blush yet again. Thankfully, Maria had left the dining area, or she might have seen it and understood that I couldn't help thinking about my pink babydoll nightgown, about the bow on my chest, and about how the indulgence of the cake would help me fill out the curves the nightgown was designed to flatter and enhance.

For him. The richness of the sponge cake and the heavenly creaminess of the frosting practically overwhelmed my senses. I had to close my eyes, but behind their lids I saw a bedroom, and me in it, in the nightgown.

Nothing but the nightgown—he didn't allow me even to wear panties... not even the thong panties from the top drawer. He... he liked me that way, completely bare under the sheer fabric, with the bow on my chest that presented my breasts... my tits... melons... to him as a present.

He... his face was shadowed, but one of his big hands reached out to hold my big breasts. The other went behind me to take hold of my bottom... my ass. It had gotten bigger, but his hand was bigger still, and he held me right in the center, under the nightgown's hem, so that he could work his middle finger between the cheeks and...

I licked the spoon. I thought of him kissing me then whispering that I must kneel down... that he had something else for me to lick... that even though I had never done that before, I would learn now... that he had paid Selecta a lot of money to make sure they would make me into the kind of girl who sucked men's cocks and did it well...

"Isabella," Maria said, "finish up that cake, please."

I pulled the spoon from my mouth, realizing that the sensor between my legs had undoubtedly given me away, though at least I hadn't let my hand drift under the table and inside the nightgown. I looked at Maria nevertheless as if she hadn't caught me doing or thinking anything unusual.

Then I looked down at the three remaining bites of cake on my plate. I should have felt stuffed, but instead I felt perfectly satisfied and...

I frowned. Between my eyes and the plate—had my breasts grown in the last *two minutes?*

I spent the rest of the day watching rom-coms in my room. I tried not to look down at my breasts in the pink nightgown more than once every five minutes, but with nothing else to distract me but the screen, it proved very difficult—and I couldn't seem to keep my hand from traveling to my backside either. They didn't seem to be growing as the hours went by, but I still couldn't figure out whether I had added a millimeter or two at the table, eating the cake.

Watching on my big bed, curled on my side, I had to turn onto my back and sit up so that I wouldn't keep squeezing my bottom through the sheer fabric. That meant that my eyes strayed more often to my chest, but eventually the movies distracted me enough that I could keep my eyes on the screen.

I wasn't really a rom-com girl, but I had found them soothing in the past. Today—understandably, I thought— the characters and the plots, familiar and even tired as they were, brought me to sympathetic, happy tears.

The modern-day prince who only needed the right commoner from America made my heart swell with wistful joy when he kissed his bride-to-be for the first time. The scowling billionaire who bumped into the hard-bitten young newspaper reporter at Christmas and changed her life anonymously, before she figured out it was him and made public all his charity, turning him into a year-round Santa Claus and winning his heart...

I sobbed with vicarious happiness even as I wished for my own prince, my own Santa, my own...

I bit my lip as the credits rolled on *Everyday Santa*. I didn't even want to let the word into my mind right now, because it would bring too much emotion.

Sponsor. I felt my brow furrow as those thoughts refused to stop. *Husband.*

I remembered a moment in the movie when the billion-aire had looked like he might get a little annoyed with the reporter. I remembered how my heart had jumped at the fierce expression on the actor's face... how I had felt an embarrassing tingle between my thighs.

Husband. I felt a frown furrow my brow. *A wealthy man with a firm hand.*

My lips had parted, and my breathing had started to become labored. What the fuck was wrong with me?

Someone knocked on my door. I started violently as the sharp noise interrupted my reverie, my eyes going to the door, expecting it to open the way it would if it was a doctor or nurse outside. Instead, after a pause of a few seconds, they knocked again.

Puzzled, realizing the knocker meant to give me the chance to prepare myself and even to refuse to let them in, I called out, "Just a moment."

Flustered but also a little grateful to whoever stood in the hall for this token of respect for my privacy, I closed my laptop and stood up from the bed. My breathing felt a little heavy and my right foot had gone partially to sleep. I looked down at the nightgown and my eyes went wide as I struggled to figure out whether my bust was the same size it had been when I lay down.

I resisted the urge to hold my breasts, to weigh them in my hands and try to see whether I could figure it out. I did my best to forget about the embarrassing nightgown and its bow, about not having anything on underneath it. I walked to the door and opened it.

Instantly, I became almost painfully aware of my body and the pink babydoll in which my prospective sponsor had dressed me. The man who stood there in a dark business suit regarded me in a way that told me who he was before he had said a word.

He had put me in this frilly little nightgown with the pink bow on the front. My brain scrambled desperately for his name, but as soon as it came to my lips... *Carl Thring... Mr. Thring...* my brain screamed at me *not* to say it—not to give this... this... asshole the satisfaction of seeing that I had recognized him instantly despite never having seen him before.

I couldn't deny him the horrid, evident satisfaction of the blood that flooded my cheeks.

His sheer handsomeness made that impossible. His impeccable dark beard, his square jaw under it, his piercing gaze.

He's better looking than either of the guys in the rom-coms, I realized as I felt my lips part, and *Mr. Thring?* almost emerged from them.

I supposed I should have expected the conflict in my mind and my body over whether to acknowledge that my so-called "prospective sponsor" stood in the doorway of this pink bedroom. After I had reacted so strongly to the movies, in the wake of the humiliating moments when Maria had come to get me and when I had eaten that fucking cake… well, I should have realized that whatever Selecta's product development team had started going in my body was having a strange effect on my brain as well.

I didn't, though. Not at that point, because the man who had written that lewd note and given me this intimate present before he had even met me now confronted me here. The idea that he could just saunter into the presumably top-secret Selecta research facility and knock on my door made me just stand there, thinking about his eyes on my body, watching their gaze travel up and down as he waited for me to say something.

"Mr. Thring?"

I figured out that the words had come out of my mouth a full second after I had said them. Or so it seemed to me, anyway—like my lips and tongue and vocal cords had taken on a separate life of their own. Like my body had decided to speak in the timid little voice I heard, meekly asking the tall, slim, unbearably handsome older man in front of me if he was indeed the prospective sponsor who wanted to… to…

Fuck me. He wants to fuck me like… like the kind of girl who has a bow on her pink nightgown to let a man know he should use her as he pleases.

CHAPTER 12

 *sabella*

"Hello, Isabella," Mr. Thring said.

For some reason I could only think about my hands. I looked down at them and saw that I had raised them in front of my breastbone—in front of the bow, really, as if I might keep him from seeing that and thus defend my whole body from his piercing eyes.

Realizing I had now taken several seconds to respond in any way to his greeting, I looked up again, both wanting—needing—to see those eyes once more and fearing that sight, and what it might do to me. Chocolate brown: *dark* chocolate brown, like the really, really good stuff that's almost too bitter, but turns your palate into gold if you let it warm up in your mouth.

And... I felt a new flush in my face and down below... *possessive* or maybe *acquisitive*. Those eyes, I suddenly thought, rarely looked at anything their owner couldn't purchase, if he hadn't already purchased it.

As I watched, the slight smile he had worn since I had opened the door, the little turning up of the left corner of his mouth, changed. His perfect lips broadened inside the neat beard, and I saw his even more perfect, gleaming white teeth as his face broke into a dazzling smile.

"It's okay," he said. "I know how nervous you are. I'm just here to say hello today and to talk about what happens next."

My lips parted as my brain worked through the implications—the shameful implications, as they seemed to me—of this information.

Today... meaning Mr. Thring would return—that this visit represented the first of several... of *many*, even...

To do... what? I felt my brow furrow as I thought of the big bed, of the big bathroom.

Just here to say hello. Future visits would involve... what?

Talk about what happens next. Yes, that I felt I could be into. Among other things, talk about how I would rather not have a prospective sponsor. Or... maybe how if I *did* have a prospective sponsor—one named Carl Thring—I would want to make certain he understood that *I* would call the shots.

Maybe I wouldn't mind wearing lingerie he sent me. Maybe I wouldn't even mind intimacy with him (to use the word all Selecta Arrangements girls did for sex), but the whole *I'm in charge of you* vibe he gave off wouldn't work for me.

I swallowed hard and found my voice at last. "Okay," I said. "Um, maybe we could go talk in the lounge?"

He tilted his head to the side a bit. The way the simple gesture made the light from the hallway fall across his chiseled cheekbones distracted me so completely that I almost forgot what I had just said. My hands folded themselves into loose fists as a mortifying tremor passed through my whole body.

To my dismay, he noticed it—he clearly noticed just about everything going on around him. The sheer intelligence in his face, the way it implied that I, Isabella Stanford, had accomplished something in attracting his attention, made me feel a little dizzy.

"No," he said. "We'll talk here in your room. I guess I misled you a bit when I said I'm just here to say hello. I'm also going to get a good look at how you're coming along, and it's much more convenient to do that in private."

My lips parted with what I knew should be some protest —maybe not defiance or rebellion, but at least a *no* to the idea that he could just knock on my door and then enter my bedroom. Could I call for Maria? For Dr. Hethcote or the tech?

Could I even say *no* at all, or would the nurse or the doctor just summon Joe the security guard to put me over his knee again, and make me let Mr. Thring in.

Or... would Mr. Thring himself...

I looked down at his hands. I couldn't help it. They hung at his sides, neatly manicured. Not dinner-plate sized like Joe's but very big, the fingers long and strong. My breathing sped up through my open mouth.

"I'm allowed to discipline you, Isabella," he said.

I looked up into his face, my eyes and my mouth both wide open and my heart racing, to see that he must have read my mind—must have seen me looking at his hands and known precisely why I had. "I should say that I know you got spanked earlier today. I watched it on the video feed Selecta provided me with."

"I…" My voice faltered. I had managed to speak, but only the single monosyllable, and the weak sound of my voice only made my face get hotter. I felt tears forming at the corners of my eyes. I had meant to say *I didn't.* Just a ridiculous reflex, trying to ward off embarrassment with a stupid lie.

I realized I hadn't even really processed what he had said before he revealed that he had *watched* me getting spanked over the security guard's knee. That part had seemed bad enough. But before that…

"You're allowed to…" More words, but just as mortifying.

"To discipline you," he said, nodding. "Why don't we avoid that, and I can explain once you've let me in. I should say that you also don't have to consent to me coming into your bedroom. Just like I can punish you if I want, I can also just grab you and carry you inside and lock the door behind us."

My body... the body whose strange differences from the one inside which I had woken up that morning, back in my apartment I felt even more strongly at this horrid moment... it responded with a thrill of unwelcome arousal so strong that my knees literally went weak, and I felt myself begin to fall.

Mr. Thring reached out to catch me, and I knew that he didn't mean me any harm—I could even see the compassionate look in his eyes. The feeling that I *wanted* him to catch me, needed him to touch me, made me do the complete opposite. I took a step back, and due to the simple physics of the situation—wobbly knees, gravity, moving foot—I did fall down.

Right on my ass, in my pink babydoll nightgown. *His* pink babydoll nightgown, with my thighs splayed and the hem raised to my waist. I cried out in abject shame as I looked up at him, knowing what he could see, how good a view he had of my bare pussy. My flight reflex took over. I scrambled to turn over and got on my hands and knees, and despite the voice yelling *You look ridiculous* in my head, I started to crawl away from my prospective sponsor.

I felt ridiculous too. I got to the bed, some wild idea in my head that I could cower in the corner between it and the wall and fend him off until... until what? Until Joe the security guard came, carrying one of the frightening implements from the discipline room, to help Mr. Thring hold me down, so he could...

I heard the door close behind him. I remembered what he had said about locking it, and I realized that I hadn't noticed anything resembling a bolt or a button on it. Nevertheless, I did hear a distinct click. It made me turn my head to look fearfully at Mr. Thring as he stood a foot or so inside the room, putting his handheld back into the breast pocket of his suit coat.

"I've locked the door, just as I said," he told me, his voice matter-of-fact. "It won't open again until I'm ready to unlock it. Before that happens, we're going to come to an understanding, Isabella."

I stared at him, my heart pounding and my mind racing. If he could lock and unlock my door that way, remotely, what did that mean for me? What did it say about this "treatment"?

Mr. Thring leaned back against the door, looking utterly at his ease in the pink bedroom I had so quickly come to think of as mine. He put his hands in his pockets.

"So..." I said, groping desperately for something to say. "So what do I need..."

The broad smile that had disappeared for a few moments returned. "What do you need to do to get me to leave?" he said.

Mutely, feeling ever more foolish there on the floor on my hands and knees, I nodded.

"Let's start by having you stand up and having a seat on your bed. Then I'm going to go sit in the chair by the vanity, and we're going to have a chat."

As he spoke, the smile faded in wattage to suit the serious tone with which he conveyed this instruction, but his handsome face remained pleasant and unthreatening. I felt my brow pucker as I contemplated obeying his wishes. The part of me that still resisted the idea of doing anything at all according to this man's desires seemed to grow weaker by the moment.

Reasonable. Wealthy. Gorgeous.

I started to get up, feeling as if for the first time the silkiness of the sheer nightgown rustling around my hips and my bottom. Self-consciously, I put my hands down to try to hold it in place, my modesty suddenly taking over—and flaring up much more strongly as I felt how smoothing the fabric down pulled it tighter over my newly fuller breasts.

When I looked over at Mr. Thring again, still leaning against the wall, the bigger smile had come back onto his face. My breath caught in my throat. Something else had appeared in that dazzling expression, something new. I understood instantly that he must have noticed exactly what I had: the way my chest looked in the pretty night-gown he had given me, underneath the bow and accentuated by it.

Heat flashed into my face. I tried to force my features into the *who cares* sneer, hoping that the expression itself would change the mortifying reaction of my body.

But that reaction—the mingled alarm in my tummy, the embarrassment in my face, and the lewd need in my stiff nipples and tingling clit—proved much too strong. Knowing this man had his eyes all over me, that he felt he had the right to inspect me that way, and that he meant to *keep* looking at me this way... I had to move my eyes down to his feet, where his gleaming dress shoes seemed to epitomize both his wealth and the power over me it had given him.

I sat on the bed, feeling small and helpless. I put my hands in my lap and looked at them. I sensed him moving, drawing nearer, and for the first time I realized how big a man Mr. Thring was. As big as Joe the security guard, really, though not beefy in the same way. Mr. Thring moved like a lion rather than like an ox.

At the edge of my vision, I saw him pull the chair out from the vanity, lift it into the air and turn it around so deftly it looked like a magic trick. Then I saw all of him, from the chest down coming into view as he sat, his knees a foot away from mine. The contrast between his sharply-creased pants and my bare knees seemed so dramatic that it sent a new wave of heat to my cheeks all by itself.

"Look at me, please, Isabella," his deep voice said.

I didn't. I couldn't. I kept staring down at my fingers as they twined themselves, seemingly of their own accord, in my pink lap, pressed tightly down there as if to keep away the unwelcome feelings Mr. Thring had brought with him into my bedroom. I scrunched my eyes so that I could barely see my prospective sponsor's knees.

I heard him sigh, and then he said, his voice much firmer, "I told you to look at me."

I still didn't want to, but suddenly I found that no matter what my brain said, my body couldn't disobey. I looked up, my eyes going wide at the bizarre, disorienting feeling that he, and not I, was in control of what my muscles did.

"There we go," he said, the smile gone from his lips. "That's what Selecta is calling the *Voice of Authority*. I don't want to have to use it often, but I will if it's necessary to get you to listen."

arl

I hadn't expected I would use the voice of authority at all. It had frankly seemed a little monstrous even in Selecta's marketing materials.

One feature of RELM we're proud to offer you as a diamond-level member is the Voice of Authority. *Thanks to Selecta's proprietary, cutting-edge DNA editing techniques, our RELM researchers have recently unlocked the limbic system of the human brain to a previously undreamt-of extent. You'll be the beneficiary, when it comes to getting what you want, and are entitled to it, out of your new Selecta Arrangements relationship with your RELM girl.*

I studied Isabella's face, frowning a little at the shock I saw there. Selecta's marketers had predicted that.

When you use the voice for the first time, your RELM girl will probably not understand what just happened. Indeed, her first reaction to your ability to command her body as you choose will almost certainly be negative. Our data says that it takes a young woman undergoing RELM therapy three to five uses of the voice by her sponsor to become accustomed to the feeling.

Isabella had opened her mouth halfway, and I thought I could tell that she—out of sheer instinct—was trying to see if she could even speak. Like a pretty, wild creature caught in a net, her body tested the limits of its unwelcome restraint.

A deep blush spread across her cheeks too and brought to my mind the most intriguing part of the e-brochure Selecta had sent me.

Remember, though, that the voice's effect can only cause compliance in cases where the young woman already wishes to comply because of her submissive needs. She might never be able to admit it, but you will probably see evidence that doing what you've commanded, distressing or shameful as it may be, is in fact part of her psychological and physiological makeup.

Don't hesitate to use it! She'll be happier in the end, just as you will. We've already taken your voiceprint, so all you'll need to do is lower your tone a minor third and tell your girl what to do. Her subconscious will take painless control of her body, and she'll obey, frequently without knowing that your instructions only represent what she truly wants.

Click here to the calibration tool, which will teach you precisely how to pitch your vocal timbre.

Bemused and not supposing I would use the voice as reflexively as I had just done in Isabella's bedroom, I had clicked and spent five minutes training myself to deliver commands. When, a few moments ago, the time had come to make use of it, the words had just come out in the proper tone.

When I had understood that my voice's pitch matched the necessary timbre, I had felt certain that it wouldn't work —that despite all Selecta's technological advances, we couldn't be living in the sci-fi world this *Voice of Authority* seemed to come from. Then Isabella had looked up.

For an instant I had thought the movement had come of her own accord—that her conscious mind had wanted to obey. Then I had seen the startlement in her eyes and the blush across her cheeks.

Her mouth closed and then opened, and then she actually tried to speak.

"The...?" She frowned, apparently surprised that she actually could say what she wanted, after I had just made her look up when she had expected to keep looking down. "The what?"

Isabella

Mr. Thring looked intently at me. His dark eyes seemed unreadable.

"The voice of authority," he repeated. "Usually they just call it *the voice*. That's what we'll call it, you and I, when I have to use it to help you obey me."

My heart started to race—really race, as if it were trying to outbeat every other heart on the planet. At the same time, the heat in my face seemed to rise in order of magnitude because, worst of all, down below, under the sheer, silky fabric of the pink nightgown, it seemed like an even bigger fire had just flared up.

To my horror, my folded hands, still in my lap, couldn't keep from pushing down.

I watched Mr. Thring's eyes go downward, and I knew he had noticed the movement. My mouth opened, and my brain scrambled for some lie, but it was just too much. I felt my face crumple into tears. I tried to look somewhere else but into his eyes, but I found that the horrible *voice* thing made it impossible. I had to keep looking at Mr. Thring.

I wanted to scream as well as sob, but the worst part of it —worse even than not being able to look away when I wanted to—lay in how I felt, way at the back of my mind, that whatever his words had done to me, they hadn't truly made me do anything against my will.

Something in me *wanted* to do as he said. Something even took *pride* in continuing to obey him, continuing to look into his face as he looked down at my hands, helplessly trying to stimulate my aching clit. It was shameful, but maybe… maybe that was why he'd made me do it.

Maybe it's why I really want *to do it.*

A full sob burst from my throat.

Mr. Thring raised his eyes to mine. "Why don't you stand up and come over here?" he said gently. At the bottom of my field of vision I watched him splay his big thighs in the beautifully tailored pants. I saw it in my imagination, me getting up and going to stand between my prospective sponsor's knees. Still looking right at him, I shook my head.

He spoke again, and his voice sounded deeper.

"Come here, Isabella," he said.

It took a moment for me to realize that my limbs had started to move, that I had raised myself from the bed, still looking right into his eyes. Then I put it together, and I let out another sob as I obeyed my sponsor—how could I keep calling him *prospective* now? Again, the worst part was that I knew... *knew*... deep down... that I did it because I wanted to.

What does 'I' mean, anyway? The strange, disorienting thought swam into view before I could force it away. *When you're apparently at war with yourself?*

I—my body, anyway, and the part of me that seemed to have taken root since this morning—stepped hesitantly toward Mr. Thring. He had his knees fully spread now, and his big hands lay on his thighs. I couldn't really look at them, though I very much wanted to. His command to give my attention to his face still seemed to have an unbreakable hold on me.

His eyes smiled. When I understood that he had the kind of brow, the kind of cheek-muscles that could do that, just suddenly show you that he felt pleasure or satisfaction at my obedience, my heart skipped a beat.

Oh, fuck. I had just met him. Only what? Five minutes ago? Yes, I had had his note in the back of my mind for the past three hours—and they had made me put on this distracting pink nightgown and wear it all day. And, yes, as a Selecta Arrangements girl I had gotten used to progressing to intimacy within the space of an hour or two—even if I had always said no sex until the second date and kept that rule through all my years of sponsor-hunting.

But... this man...

Was it his obvious wealth? His clear intelligence? His voice—even when he didn't use whatever horrible ability Selecta had given him to control my physical movements?

Wait... I felt a frown come over my face. Mr. Thring's voice definitely wasn't the one I had heard in the booth, but... it also definitely resembled it in some vague but very important way. A shiver went through my body. I had to keep looking into his much-too-handsome face, but I felt like my knees might buckle under me before I crossed even the remaining six inches that would bring me between my sponsor's legs.

"P-please..." I said. "May I...?"

"Call me *sir*," Mr. Thring said very softly. He didn't use the voice, but the same part of me seemed to respond to his shameful, thrilling words as he evoked when he did lower his timbre and give me an order.

"Sir," I breathed. "May I look down? Please?"

The smile in his eyes went to his lips.

"Yes, Isabella," he said. "You may look down."

A tiny whimper emerged from my throat. My nipples, my clit, my pussy itself had responded to his mercy so forcefully that for a moment the wobbling of my knees increased instead of decreasing, and I started to stumble. The moment I looked down at his right hand—the one he would use to discipline me, I thought—it began to come up, and I knew my sponsor would steady me before I fell.

I cried out at the mere idea that Mr. Thring would now touch me for the first time, and then my whole body jerked as he did, his hands under my arms steadying me, but also holding me there, much too close to my breasts.

My even larger breasts, I suddenly realized. They had grown again, somehow, in the last two minutes. They felt very big, heavy even, under my new sponsor's hands.

"Oh my God," I whispered.

"What is it?" I heard Mr. Thring's voice ask. His tone sounded a tiny bit teasing, but his words also sounded sympathetic, even compassionate for my distress.

My gaze had descended to the notch of his collarbone, where I could see in the open neck of his crisp white button-down shirt. A few curly hairs peeked out there, and they made my forehead furrow at the simple differ-ence between a man's chest and a woman's, between a fortyish billionaire and a thirty-year-old Selecta Arrange-ments girl looking for a man to take care of her.

I raised my eyes to look him in the face again, feeling a new blush spread on my cheeks as I did it voluntarily, in desperate search of something in my sponsor's expres-sion. I had managed to stand firmly on my feet, but Mr. Thring still had his hands beneath my arms, his thumbs resting lightly atop what suddenly felt like a shelf of pillowy flesh.

He looked back at me with a little smile that had in it something of the satisfied, possessive air I had seen earlier, which made my tummy flip over, but something also of kindness and sympathy. My forehead furrowed more deeply and I found that I had actually taken my lower lip between my teeth, like a girl in a romcom.

"My..." I said, and then the heat in my face made me stop. I looked down at them. B cups, now? Definitely—maybe even a little bigger.

The worst part was that I desperately, desperately wanted them touched. I wanted to do it myself, I wanted to weigh them in my hands and figure out what they felt like, on my fingers, but even more inside my chest. The very thought sent a wave of arousal crashing through me.

Much, much, more, though, and to my dismay—even to my horror—I wanted *him* to do it.

I looked up at him, willing him to do it and willing him not to. Inside me, whatever changes to my mind the bizarre therapy session, the handles, the voice, the pill, had made seemed to press deeper into my psyche. The rational part of me screamed that this morning I never, ever would have wanted this, but even my usually logical side had to admit that, really, I just never would have *admitted* that I wanted it.

"I'm going to touch your breasts now, Isabella," said Mr. Thring. "And I'm going to tell you about our arrangement."

 _sabella_

I let out a helpless little cry as he did as he had promised. He put his hands on them, over them, turned a little to the side so that his finger went underneath. Mr. Thring's hands were big enough that they could still comfortably hold all of my breasts, but I had a sensation very different from what I had experienced with any man before. For the very first time I felt someone _heft_ my... my...

Boobs. I have boobs. That thought by itself made me chew on the inside of my cheek because my hips had just jerked and, most distracting of all, my pussy had just clenched, hard.

I'm sure that a lot of girls would have said that, technically, I had had boobs before. The little protrusions that had represented my excuse for breasts from the age of nineteen on, however, had never seemed to me a good fit for the word. I had always felt certain that no man would ever describe them that way.

Now I knew for sure that Mr. Thring, when talking to a billionaire friend about how he had bought a girl for his pleasure, maybe even to take to the altar and ensure she would remain in his bed as long as he pleased, might well tell him about her big boobs... her...

Another word floated into my mind... *rack.* He might tell his friend that his new Selecta Arrangements girl had an incredible rack.

I heard a little whimper emerge from my throat. Mr. Thring moved his thumbs underneath the satin bow that covered most of the chest of the babydoll nightgown. I gasped as they brushed over my nipples lightly and instantly stiffened them even more than his mere touch had done.

I didn't feel certain about it, but I wondered suddenly if something had happened to my nervous system as well as the tissue of my chest and backside. Did my nipples feel more sensitive than they had felt that morning?

"The treatment has heightened your responsiveness," Mr. Thring murmured, the depth of his tone seeming to vibrate into my body through his fondling hands. "They say that's a psychological thing rather than a physical one."

My breath had begun to come and go in little pants between my open lips. I swallowed hard, my mouth suddenly seeming to flood with a wetness that to my dismay I realized probably mirrored what had begun to occur between my thighs.

"I..." I said, and then I had to swallow again. "I don't... I don't understand."

"Hush," said Mr. Thring, and I felt in that new place deep in my mind that he had spoken, or really breathed with a bit of pitch, that sound in the lower register, in the voice of authority. My brow puckering, I tried reflexively to speak again, and I found I couldn't—that he had indeed stilled my voice within me.

The command hadn't stopped me from sobbing, though, or moaning, and I did. First a sob and then a moan as I reacted down below to the very idea of the voice, combined with the feeling of his hands. His touch felt muted by the fabric of the nightgown, sheer as it was, and I suddenly had the desperate urge to beg him to put his hands underneath and to touch my new boobs that way... to touch all of me that way... to feel my bottom too and tell me if he liked it.

"I think it means," he said, and the serious, level tone of his words made me raise my eyes to meet his chocolate gaze, "that you're feeling more, sexually, than you've ever felt before, because the physical changes are unlocking your submissive fantasies."

At that I tried with all my might to speak, to deny it. *I don't have submissive fantasies, you asshole. I don't. I... DO... NOT.*

The defiant part of my brain yelled it and kept yelling it. My forehead worked with the effort. My lips twitched.

I couldn't say it, and I understood more clearly than I had yet—than I had yet imagined I could understand the horrid voice—that I wasn't able to talk because some part of me didn't *want* to talk.

Because Mr. Thring had told me not to.

I let out another sob, closing my eyes against the overwhelming sensation of his hands on my breasts and the need between my thighs.

"It's time for us to come to an understanding about our arrangement," he said, his fingers moving gently, so gently on my big breasts. "Open your eyes."

He didn't use the voice, but I obeyed, because all of me knew I had to listen to him—had to figure out whether all the parts of my mind and heart could agree. Whether despite the strangeness involved, and the terror, really, all of me could at some level accept this man's sponsorship.

Sponsorship? The word had seemed applicable to my two previous sponsors. Such nice men... even, I had thought at the time, a little, you know, daddyish. Face it, someone on the forums had written once, you wouldn't be in SA if you didn't have a bit of a thing for men who liked to take charge.

BUT THAT'S NOT... NOT...

"You're going to agree to do as I say," he told me. "And I'm going to take care of you. Really, that's all."

Oh god.

His eyes... kind, but also... strict, somehow.

"Selecta is giving you the body you've always wanted."

But... no... that couldn't be what had happened...

"I want that body too. I want you, Isabella."

As he spoke, he moved his right hand down, put it boldly under the hem of the nightgown, and thrust it between my legs. The wordless command of his strong fingers made me shuffle my feet apart, so that he could touch what he wanted to touch.

I cried out. My hands flew up to hover between us, poised between pushing him away and trying to hug him.

"I want *this*," my sponsor... my master... said.

His two middle fingers entered me, so roughly that I lost my balance with the overwhelming sensation, the instant, cataclysmic descent to the brink of orgasm.

Mr. Thring's left arm wrapped around my back to keep me upright. His long fingers probed inside, curled up to touch a place I knew must be my G spot although I had never until that moment believed in its existence. My whole body seemed to spasm in his grasp, and the climax —the tremendous, irresistible feeling I hadn't even known until that morning—seemed to reach up for me, but then just as suddenly his right hand pulled out and away.

I sobbed yet again, throwing my head back and trying with all my might to press toward him, against him, into him. My hands had gone up into the air as I felt myself falling, and now I put them on Mr. Thring's shoulders, a shudder gripping my limbs at the mere touch of the fine wool, the contrast with the thin, lascivious silk in which he had dressed me.

My new sponsor's right hand hadn't gone away completely, though: I felt it come around behind me. I felt his fingers, slick with my shameful need, brush against my upper thigh as he brought them up under the lacy hem of the babydoll again. I felt him touch me there.

There. In my fleeting, mortifying fantasies, *that* part of me played a bigger role even than my breasts. I had focused on my chest, my new boobs, because they rose to my attention—literally—much more prominently than my backside did, but always at the back of my no-longer-trustworthy mind had lain my... my...

My ass. Just as I had never thought I would have boobs, I hadn't thought I could possess a true ass. Yes, I could use the term for my backside, and I acknowledged that indeed everyone has an ass of one shape or another, but... the heart-shaped, shapely, firm but prominent as a girl walked away kind of ass... the kind men look at...

The kind men like to spank and to...

He held my ass in his right hand, and I knew that until an hour or so ago he would have been able to take hold of the whole thing. Not now. Mr. Thring let out a satisfied little grunt as he took hold of the center of my bottom, where Joe the security guard had spanked me—where he himself, I knew, would enjoy disciplining me if I stepped out of line. Only the center because I had grown there just as I had grown up top.

"And *this,*" he growled into my shoulder, where my movements had pressed my body against his face.

The rumble of his voice itself sent another thrill of need shooting out from the pussy his hand had left aching. It took me a moment, though, to connect his words with what he had said before. He wanted me... my pussy... my ass... I bit my lip hard.

His middle finger pressed inward between my ass cheeks.

"Oh no," I sobbed.

He touched me there. The naughtiest place. The smallest place—still the smallest despite the changes in my body.

"And this," he said softly as the fingertip probed into the tiny flower of my anus.

I thought he would take it out—that he wouldn't insist on my understanding this most shameful claiming of his property. But instead he pushed in further, so that my hips bucked and I tried to move forward and away from the invading digit. I succeeded only in leaning against my sponsor more heavily, as he punished my attempt at escape by impaling me even further on his finger.

"Yes," murmured Mr. Thring. "When I think you're ready, here too. An ass this delectable is going to need regular fucking."

"Oh my God," I breathed. "You... you... can't."

"I can, though," Mr. Thring replied. The finger moved a little, in and out, and I felt my face form into a humiliating erotic pout. "I will. That's part of the understanding I want you to have."

"Oh..." I whispered. "Oh... no... please."

"Do I need to make it plainer to you, Isabella?" he asked, a little sharpness coming into his tone. Then he spoke in the lower timbre that had already begun to make my heart jump whenever I heard it, even before my brain had processed the command he would give.

"Turn around and go back to the bed and bend over it," he said in the voice of authority. "Raise your nightgown around your arms, then reach back and spread your ass for me. Show me where I'm going to fuck you when the time comes. Show me both those sweet holes where my cock goes."

I took a deep, sobbing breath. For a moment I thought I wouldn't be able to obey, because Mr. Thring would keep holding me in place, and a little shoot of joy seemed to spring up in my heart. I had supposed the thing about how really, I wanted all the things he would make me do would fade into the background of my consciousness— that I could forget about it, like some obscure piece of scientific knowledge you hear once and then lose forever.

No. As my sponsor released me from his arms and pulled the mortifying finger out of my asshole, as I turned like a robot to do as he had told me, I became fully aware of the terrible depth of need that made me obey. I didn't like it, but also, bizarrely, I took an abject kind of pride in doing as Mr. Thring said despite the utter degradation of his command.

I turned to the bed and took a step forward. I bent.

"Feet shoulder-width, please," he said, not in the voice this time. "So I can see everything."

And I did it, even though he hadn't used Selecta's horrible little trick. I did it because the man who had said he would take care of me wanted my knees apart. I moved my feet even as I pulled the nightgown up to my breasts and felt the silk brush luxuriously, erotically against my huge, dangling tits.

I reached back and took hold of the two round halves of my bottom, and I gasped as I felt how they had grown, and how unexpectedly firm they were. With a whimper of submission, I pulled them apart.

"The thing Selecta says they solved," mused Mr. Thring behind me, "is how to change a girl's skeletal structure. Apparently, the soft tissue is easy, but it took years of R and D to figure out how to widen the breastbone and the hip bone to create a work of art like your new body, Isabella."

CHAPTER 15

 _sabella_

I could feel it for myself. It made me think, semi-rationally I guess, that something in the cake—in the butter from the frosting, maybe—had packed some huge extra punch of calcium. My hips had grown wider, to match the growth of my ass. I let out a low moan at the incredibly sexy feeling, a truly womanly feeling, of my shapely cheeks under my fingers as I moved them in convulsive little tremors.

For an instant I forgot about the terrible shame, the immodesty, of showing Mr. Thring everything like that. The strangely alien feeling of my own body took hold of my consciousness, and I literally wondered for an instant if I had actually somehow gotten the wires of my nervous system crossed with some other woman's. I felt almost exactly as if I had suddenly begun to eavesdrop on another girl's thoughts.

That girl... her ideas and her feelings and her needs... a mere glimpse of them made my posture and the reality of the wealthy, handsome man behind me come crashing back into my mind.

She had bent over and raised her nightgown. At her sponsor's command, she had reached back and spread her big, heart-shaped ass so he could see her pussy and her anus.

She... *I*... had done it after he had told her, using all the most explicit, most shameful words, what he meant to do to her. How he planned to fuck her pussy and fuck her bottom-hole.

My hips jerked hard, just thinking about it. My pussy clenched even harder, and my heart jumped in horror at the sudden certainty that with all the warmth down there, my wetness would actually show itself between the pink, private lips Mr. Thring must be examining so intently.

"You were beautiful this morning, Isabella," Mr. Thring said, "and you *are* beautiful now. Your new body hasn't changed that, but like so many men I get turned on by the differences between men and women, and above all your therapy is making those differences more apparent, and..."

I whimpered as I felt his finger press gently against my anus. The sound became a long, low whine through my nose, because the finger kept pushing until it had invaded me there.

I never knew, I thought. *I never knew how embarrassing that would be, or... or how much I need it.* My face blazed with heat. I felt absolutely sure that this morning, before the pill and the booth, I would never, ever have thought that.

Or would I just never have admitted *that I thought it.*

"And just as importantly," my sponsor continued, "your therapy is helping you understand what the differences mean for you."

"Wh-what?" I breathed. "What is... what is that?"

He kept his finger inside me, inside my most private place, but I felt it shift a little and turn, as I sensed him standing up behind me. I heard a sound that I couldn't place for a second, a sort of crinkling, and then I realized with a rush and my whole backside contracted with another hard clench of my aching sheath. He had unzipped his fly.

"They mean," he said slowly, as if he savored every word, "that you need to serve a man like me with this luscious body of yours. You need it every minute of every day."

I gasped. He had taken the finger out and put *it*... him... his hardness... his rigid cock between my bottom cheeks. His hands, over my own, pressed the round halves together around the enormous shaft, and he thrust gently back and forth. From behind and above me, I heard Mr. Thring let out a little murmur of satisfaction, as if the valley that cleft my bottom, enlarged and deepened for him, had given him an unexpectedly great pleasure. What felt like the hottest blush of my life turned my face so crimson, I knew, that I felt grateful he had bent me over my bed this way to do the humiliating thing.

"It's not... it's not *true*," I said, but the words came out in a little moan that seemed instantly to betray their meaning as a lie.

He didn't bother to respond to my denial. Instead, his words seemed like a reply to what my mind, having apparently become uncontrollably wanton in the last few hours, really meant, and had really begun to beg for.

"I'm not allowed to fuck you today," he said.

The remaining dignity in my spirit and the shreds of rationality in my mind did everything they could to stop it, but I whimpered. I whined like a puppy denied a treat.

"I'm allowed to let you come, though, Isabella, if you're a good girl."

Another humiliating whimper emerged from my throat.

"And of course I'm going to come myself, even though I'll probably make this nightgown very difficult to clean."

For a moment he fell silent, still thrusting gently up and down the hot groove of my backside, taking his ease there as the little grunts of satisfaction rumbling out of his chest so clearly indicated.

Then he spoke, his words so clear and precisely chosen that I felt certain he meant to humiliate me with them as deeply as possible... that he understood much better than I the terrible need for degradation that had somehow come fully awake in me today.

"Selecta thinks you've probably never sucked a cock, my dear. Obviously, they know everything you've done in your apartment, and they tell me that your sponsors were kind enough never to make you. What they can't tell me, of course, is what your experience was before you joined Selecta Arrangements, or what your sponsors perhaps made you do in a taxi or a restaurant bathroom. Your profile tells me that neither of them was really that kind of guy."

Through this utterly mortifying speech, I felt the little tremor in my hips and in my knees, which had begun when his finger had first pressed against my smallest place, take over completely. Desperate for a touch between my thighs to accompany the degrading stimulation of my sponsor's words, I moved with the sliding motion of his hardness between my round cheeks. I had my eyes tightly shut, as if I could block out the fantasy images... the non-memories of a man forcing my head down in the back seat of a cab... making me kneel in a toilet stall.

"So," he said, "have you, Isabella? Have you ever sucked a man's penis the way a good girl—or to be sure, a bad one —does?"

Something about that contrast, the one that Mr. Thring had just playfully denied—good girl, bad girl—got to me in a new way. My sheer submissive need had seemed only a moment before to have put the rebellion in my heart and mind to flight forever. Suddenly it became available and it surged back up inside me as I thought about *good* and *bad.*

I gritted my teeth, and I didn't answer. I felt my limbs tense against him, my backside tightening in protest under my hands—and under his much bigger hands covering them, firmly gripping my cheeks.

It might not matter to *him* whether I considered myself a good girl or a bad girl, but it mattered to *me.* Not in some shitty old-fashioned patriarchal way, where your minister or your teacher or even your mommy says you're a good girl for saying your prayers or doing your homework or putting away your clothes—or a bad one for cursing, or cheating, or leaving the clothes on the floor.

Or a school principal says you're a bad girl for sucking off the captain of the football team in a deserted classroom.

Or your husband says you're a good girl because as shameful as you know it is, you kneel down in front of him and accept his huge manhood into your mouth, let him fuck your face until he pulls out his cock and spurts his come on your big tits in the pink silk and the satin bow.

Not that way... that stuff might distract me, sure, but the old-fashioned *good* label and the antiquated *bad* label didn't *matter* to me. Not the way my ability to do the opposite—to free myself from stupid labels when I thought about who I wanted to be—mattered.

My head reared up as I tried to move my hands and straighten up and found I couldn't. For the blink of an eye I had supposed that the defiance rising in me would do away with the power of the fucking voice of authority thing, but no.

Open war broke out inside me. My memory told me that only a minute ago—if that, even—I had acknowledged that this *voice* shit wouldn't have worked on me if I didn't actually, deep down, want to obey this asshole. Now I saw that there might be some part of me—okay, some deep-seated part of me, even—that did fantasize about... obedience and... submission.

I didn't have to give in, though. He could make me do things with my body, sure, but it had become clear that he didn't control my thoughts. I could reject the labels, the goodness and the badness alike, inside where it mattered. My wanton desires might be deep seated, but couldn't my mind keep them in check from above?

Deep seated. That part fired a shot across my defiant mind's bow. A tremor of hot, shameful need traveled through my whole body, seeming to feed off the tension my resistance had generated as I tried to defy Mr. Thring's command even as he used my own seat to pleasure his hardness, moving his erection up and down that newly deep valley. The one Selecta had deepened, for him, so my body would provide more enjoyment to my master.

141

"Answer me, Isabella. Have you had a man's penis in your mouth?"

I heard it—my *body* heard it—the sound of the words, as if they had come from above—which of course they literally had. Above me and behind me, from the man to whom my body had made itself available, exposed all my most intimate, most embarrassing secret places.

My brain recognized the voice, and the conflict between mind and body brought more tension to my limbs as the conflict raged on. I felt my face contort with the pressure of one element of my psyche trying to stop the other from using my mouth and my vocal cords to obey my sponsor's command.

"N-no," I choked out. *I?* Had *I* spoken the monosyllable— or had something else, someone else spoken through me? I had the very odd thought that I *should* feel like I was going crazy, but in fact I actually felt saner, despite the ongoing war inside…

Inside what? My totality? My identity? I didn't know, but I realized that I knew how to ask the question, at least. Heat rose in my cheeks as I understood that I had Selecta, and Mr. Thring, to thank for the unwelcome but undeniable self-knowledge.

"Well," he said, speaking in his normal timbre as I felt him step back, his cock leaving my ass feeling strange and his hands remaining, turning to mold my bare, rounded cheeks possessively. "If Selecta tells me the truth, you'll learn very quickly. Stand up and turn around."

I remained where I was. He hadn't used the voice. For a moment I wondered whether he had forgotten to drop the pitch of his words, but then I felt certain he hadn't. He wanted me to obey without his having to resort to the degrading ability Selecta had given him.

"I'll use the voice if I have to, to get what I want," he growled. "I've got your doctor's permission."

My heart thudded in my chest. Again the thrill of need that this man's dominance seemed to awaken in me every time surged between my thighs. The very idea that Dr. Hethcote had become *my* doctor filled me with indignation, but the anger only seemed to contribute to my helpless arousal.

My body desperately wanted me to be a good girl for my sponsor so I could get the reward he had promised. My mind, with equal force, cried out for me to be a bad girl instead—to disobey and to be *made* to do the shameful things Mr. Thring wanted and my flesh, transformed for his pleasure, craved.

"Are you planning to obey me, my dear?" my sponsor asked, his tone so controlled, so lightly mocking that I could see his casually raised eyebrow in my mind's eye.

"No," I said, as firmly as I could. Realizing a little belatedly that his command, even in his normal voice, to straighten up, had freed me from the previous one to bend over, I did stand up. I didn't turn around, though. Instead, I slipped away to the side, my ass coming free of his grip at last.

EMILY TILTON

Then I did turn to look at him. I put my hands out in front of me, balled into fists.

"You're going to have to use that fucking voice on me," I told him, "if you want your cock sucked."

arl

I widened my eyes a little theatrically. Down below, I felt my cock jump hard with arousal—the urgent need to fuck that newly incredible body returning. It had almost overwhelmed me when I had her bent across her bed a moment before. Her shapely ass had felt amazing on my rigid manhood, but the desire to be inside her had nearly proven too strong.

To say that Isabella Stanford looked ravishing in the pink babydoll with the satin bow put it much too mildly. The girl looked not thirty now, but a well-developed twenty-one, if that. A hot young woman coming into her curves for the first time.

Selecta had told me in their instructions for this first encounter that she almost certainly wouldn't catch on to the rejuvenating effects of the treatment for a while—a few days at least.

Remember that Isabella can't see herself from the outside, even in the mirror. We all experience our reflected physical appearance strongly in relation to our imaginary body image. She's been denying (she would say "not noticing" if you were to ask) the first signs of aging in her body for several years, so when those reverse themselves, she won't catch on immediately. You should, if you like, use that to your advantage by calling her attention, for example, to the renewed smoothness of her skin. Youth is a very potent aphrodisiac, after all.

Looking at her and remembering this advice, I decided not to call my girl's—how could I keep myself from thinking of Isabella that way?—bluff. Yes, I could certainly use the voice of authority to make her pleasure me, but it would be so much sweeter to seduce her using her own needs.

Nor did that course of action, I thought, stand in the way of exacting a little retribution for this sudden disobedience.

"Go over to the vanity, Isabella," I said quietly, stepping back a pace to clear the path and pointing to the place I meant her to move. "Put your hands on it and look at your face in the mirror."

Alarm and confusion broke out on her features, her brow creasing and her eyes growing troubled. Her lips parted as she seemed to contemplate the posture I had requested, and she clearly began to understand its possible implications.

"If I do have to use the voice, my dear, it's going to be a good deal worse for your backside," I said in the same quiet voice. "Do as I've said, please."

Her jaw dropped another millimeter. Her breath had started to come in little pants as her arousal quite obviously increased.

"Wh-what... what are you going to do?" she whispered.

I inclined my head and replied, slowly and calmly, "I'm going to discipline you for your outburst and for your foul language."

Isabella backed away, her hands stretched behind her now, until she came up against the dresser. Her desire to secure her lovely, heart-shaped ass from punishment appeared so clearly in the gesture and in her face that I almost laughed.

"Last chance," I said, raising my eyebrows. "Go to the vanity and bend over it. Look at your face in the mirror."

Isabella

I had started to chew the inside of my cheek very hard, I realized suddenly, at the salty, metallic taste of my blood.

Look in the mirror. Why? And bend over... WHY?!

If I didn't do it... if I didn't follow the apparently innocent instruction, he would use the stupid voice, and it would be worse for...

Discipline me. He just said... he just said he's going to discipline *me.*

I breathed hard, through my mouth, as I looked at him. His brown eyes looked back at me with an air of irony that made both my fear and my apparently unstoppable arousal worse. His face, his way too handsome face with that neatly trimmed beard, wore an expression that seemed steeped in an experience and a knowledge of me so thorough that it made me want to sink into the floor.

I seemed to hear the voice before I heard the words. Had my body begun to anticipate it, I wondered? Had Selecta somehow primed me in their stupid booth with that other voice that Mr. Thring's reminded me of, to do his bidding?

Or... or was I already primed? The feeling of clarity I had had a moment before, that glimpse of the dimensions of the conflict inside me, had started to slip away. For a nanosecond, I felt out of control, and then—to my dismay —the voice of authority, my master's voice, brought me out of it.

"Do as I've told you, Isabella," he said, and my body started to move, and my mind responded with gratitude, because I understood that, yes, a part of me did want to obey him —no, more accurately, *needed* to obey him.

A thought rose into my consciousness, and it made me sob, because I couldn't deny that it had come from my body and my mind had verified it.

I need discipline. I need a firm hand.

The gratitude grew despite the humiliation that came alongside it. When my sponsor used the voice, I didn't have to admit that my conscious mind would ever consent to accepting the discipline... the... the...

Punishment. That word, as it came into my brain, made my knees wobble so much, my pussy clench so hard, that I stumbled a little and I had to reach out toward the vanity top to steady myself. The mirror came up right in front of me, and I looked myself in the face, and for the first time I realized that my face had changed too—very subtly but also very definitely.

I gasped.

"You see it, don't you?" asked Mr. Thring. "The treatment is reversing the aging process too."

I would never have said that morning that my face had lines or the skin had gotten saggy. I was only thirty, for God's sake. But I could indeed see it. I looked twenty again, fresh-faced, though without any of the lingering acne I had had at that age.

I looked, well, fucking gorgeous.

And... Mr. Thring had chosen to sponsor me... he had dressed me in this nightgown that set off my new figure and my new face and made me look movie-star sexy—

more conventionally attractive than I had ever thought I could be.

His left hand, behind my back, started suddenly to do something that my limbic system recognized as alarming before I even understood what the action might involve. I started to turn around, to try both to see and to shy away, but my sponsor's hand proved too quick. He had raised the back of the nightgown and pressed its gathered hem against the small of my back before I could do anything at all—and when I tried to struggle, feeling his strength holding me in place, I found that the command he had given me and then reinforced with the voice of authority, to come to the vanity and bend over it, kept me there.

I felt him shift a little, to my left side, and then I felt his other hand on my bottom. I gave a startled cry because he had something in it, something smooth and thin and supple.

Oh. No. His belt. It could only be his belt—I hadn't noticed him taking it off, but...

"Yes, Isabella," he said into my ear. "It's my belt. When you disobey me from now on, you'll feel it across your backside."

"Oh God," I whispered, the emotions and sensations, the thoughts and feelings, roiling in my chest, my belly, my pussy... too many to pull apart and look at...all of them seeming to flow from the feeling of the leather against my bottom-cheeks.

"This is what happens to young ladies when they're naughty and don't respect their sponsors' instructions."

His voice sounded terribly even and calm, as if he merely meant to tell me how the world worked. Young ladies who belonged to wealthy men, who had had their aging reversed so that they became young ladies again, sucked men's cocks on command. Or they received a whipping—and then, I knew without Mr. Thring telling me, they did kneel down and take their sponsor's hardness between their lips.

"No," I said. "Please." Fear of the belt, of the agony it would visit upon my backside, seemed to paralyze me. The now-familiar struggle between the voice's command and my mind's wishes set my whole body trembling.

The belt moved against my ass, caressing my cheeks down low, moving to my upper thighs. I had my lower lip between my teeth, and a tiny whimper emerged. My breathing came in quick snorts through my nose, and my heart had started to go a mile a minute.

Mr. Thring spoke softly. "I'm going to give you a choice, Isabella," he said into my ear. "In a moment, I'm going to release you from the voice of authority."

"What?" I gasped, a new kind of panic filling my chest.

"I'm still going to keep you in place here, by force if I have to. You're going to have a whipping either way, and you're going to suck my cock either way, but if you want to have your whipping while you learn to suck a man's penis, I would be happy to combine your lessons, and I will punish you less severely than I would if I gave them to you separately. And, of course, you'll receive your reward only when you show me you can be a good girl."

I had closed my eyes, and my mouth had opened so that my breath could come in and out of it. The feeling of his left hand pressing on my back and the belt's smooth leather rubbing up and down, back and forth, made it impossible to think at all, let alone with the degree of clarity I had seemed to attain a few moments earlier.

"You may move as you like, my dear," he said, but his hands remained on me. The one with the belt shifted so that with the cool metal buckle in his palm, his fingers fondled my bottom, the tips pressing where I knew he could find my mortifying wetness if he pushed a little further. My need—my new body's helpless response to his arrogance and his casual possessiveness, his apparent willingness to use a firm hand with me when he decided I needed it.

At one and the same time, my mind screamed *I don't!* and my body screamed *I do!*

My body had control of my limbs, but my brain's rejection of the idea that I would simply accept this humiliating state of affairs somehow got into my nervous system and made me try desperately to get away from the vanity and from the hands and from the belt.

I pushed on the polished wooden surface, but Mr. Thring's hand pushed down hard. I sensed him tightening his grip on the fabric of the nightgown, as if to make sure it wouldn't fall down to keep my backside from getting all the punishment I had coming to it.

I cried out in fear even before I heard the crack and felt the burning line across my right ass-cheek. Then I cried out again louder, and I struggled harder, flailing out with my arms so that my sponsor had to wrap his left arm around my waist even as he continued to whip me.

"No... no... please," I sobbed. Three more lashes had fallen. My bottom felt as if he had laid burning brands across it. "I'll... I'll..."

He stopped whipping me. "Yes, my dear?" he asked.

A surge of resistance tried to rise in my mind, but as soon as he had stopped whipping me the ache between my thighs seemed to grow into a fire even more raging than the pain in my bottom. I had resisted too—I hadn't just given in, right?

"I'll suck it," I sobbed. "Please let me suck it."

 *sabella*

As I heard the humiliating words emerge from my mouth —*please let me suck it*—I literally had no idea where in me they had come from. For a moment I actually wondered first whether there was another girl in the room and then whether Selecta had somehow put someone else's personality inside my mind alongside my own.

Then, more quickly this time because I had started to become used to these conflicting feelings, my brain put it together. No, *I* had said it. *I* had just begged to suck the cock of a man I had met only a few minutes before.

Somewhere in the back of my mind I recognized that the war inside me had gotten more violent, but also that this heightening represented not a troubling thing but actually from a crucial perspective, a good one. The things I had deep down, which had made me feel out of control earlier that day, with Maria and then with Joe the security guard, the things that had put me over his knee for the first spanking of my life—the mortifying Selecta treatment had brought them to the surface, and I could see them for the first time.

No, the therapy had helped *me* bring them to the surface.

And...

Mr. Thring let me pull away and turn to the side and kneel down. I looked up at him from the floor. *He* had helped too. I felt my face pucker as my cheeks flared up again into burning heat to match the lingering sear of the belt across my ass-cheeks. He had helped, sending me this nightgown out of my fantasies... calling me beautiful... so clearly wanting me and yet—unlike any man I had ever met before—able to hold back, able to take his time and to dominate me properly.

Wealthy. Powerful. He looked down at me with desire in his eyes and nevertheless also with reserve. He meant to fuck me, to possess me, to enjoy me. But he meant to do it on his own terms and those alone. With his firm hand... his belt... the enormous cock he started to take out again, to stroke so arrogantly right in front of me... he would have me just as he chose and in no other way.

Out of the corner of my eye, because I couldn't help looking, I saw in the vanity mirror what it looked like. The submissive posture and the contrast between the silky pink babydoll nightgown and the business suit, the difference between a gorgeous, older dominant man and an equally gorgeous young woman on her knees ready to serve his pleasure... the thrill of need that broke over my body and made my pussy clench so hard between my thighs that I cried out... I thought I might hyperventilate with the speed of my breathing, but I didn't care.

He had his huge, hard penis in his left hand, and my eyes went to it, to the way he pumped it, got it ready for my mouth. In his right he had the belt still, doubled and wound around his fist. I swallowed hard as I took it in and remembered he had said he would whip me while I learned.

"Please," I whispered. "If I suck it... please don't whip me?"

I could hear it in my own voice. The submission, the terrible need for degradation, even, that hadn't been there —I would have sworn on everything holy—when I had woken up this morning.

My heart beating wildly, I looked up at Mr. Thring and saw that a smile had broken out on my sponsor's face... of satisfaction, it seemed to me, and of sheer enjoyment of the scene: his cock in his hand and a gorgeous young woman kneeling at his feet. The way my tummy flipped over, then... the way it recalled to me how badly and for how many years I had wanted to find a man who would... the way I had always put it... *take care of me.*

Watch over me.

I felt my brow furrow hard. I would have sworn on every-thing, holy or not. I would have declared to God himself that no, I didn't have a submissive bone in my body. A sob burst from my chest as part of me realized, though I knew my independent mind would continue to fight it mental tooth and mental nail, that I would have sworn falsely.

"We'll see, Isabella," he said. "Do your best, and we'll see."

"Oh my God," I breathed. "Oh no. Oh... please?"

He took a step forward. My eyes widened as his lustful smile became a different kind of expression, his brown eyes narrowing.

"Eyes down," he commanded me. "Look at my cock."

I felt a surge of gratitude in my chest, and my defiant mind despised my body for it, even as the thrill of need shot through me with the sight of Mr. Thring's big hand pumping up and down the long, rigid shaft. The round top seemed to flash at me as the circled fingers came and went.

"See how hard you got me, my dear?" he asked in a teasing voice. "See how my cock needs to be inside you?"

The arousal these words caused in every molecule of my body—that's how it felt, at least—made me shudder all over. His hand left his manhood and reached out for my chin. I shrank back in alarm, but the hold he took of my jaw felt gentle, tender even. He squeezed but only very, very softly.

"Open this," he said.

My eyes went to his other hand, the one holding the belt, as if seeking confirmation that... that I *had* to—that he would *make* me. Then I looked over again and saw the cock jutting arrogantly, obscenely out from his suit trousers. The tools of my master's dominance confronted me, and the sheer strength of his own arousal, the way my body, bought and paid for by him, turned him on.

See how my cock needs to be inside you.

I chewed on my lower lip for an instant more, and I felt his hand close a little more tightly, and then with a tiny whimper, I hesitantly parted my lips.

"Wider," said Mr. Thring. "All the way, Isabella."

My eyes darted up to his face, and I saw him frown at my disobedience. My cheeks blazed, and I lowered my gaze again, the heat spreading all through my body, throbbing between my thighs. The idea of my reward for this shameful duty, the positive reinforcement that a sponsor with a firm hand surely knew how to give, made my hips jerk.

So distracted by that need, so paralyzed by the sight of the jutting erection and the horrible belt, I kept my jaw in the same position, without willingly disobeying but knowing —yes, and fully understanding, needing—what would happen.

It happened. Mr. Thring's right hand moved, and he bent his looming body a little, at knees and waist, and he whipped me, once, twice, three times, on my right ass cheek and then on my left, and then on the right again. The lashes struck through the fabric of the nightgown, so they didn't sting as atrociously as before, but they made me cry out, and they made me open my mouth, suddenly desperate to please him.

He straightened, and he leaned forward. His huge, hard cock came closer, and a little whining sound emerged from the back of my throat as the moment, the shameful instant, approached and then became a reality. My sponsor put his rigid manhood inside my mouth. He fed it to me gently but insistently, making me receive him in reverence and submission, little by little, until my little mouth felt much too full.

Full with a humiliating, degrading morsel that I must treat with utmost respect. Feeling my forehead crease, I closed my lips a bit, and I tasted a penis for the first time, a little salty, a little acrid, and indefinably *naughty*. I was doing what bad girls do, and the thought sent a wave of arousal through my limbs that made me whimper around Mr. Thring's hardness.

Just at the little suckling movement of my lips and tongue that had let me taste him, my sponsor gave a grunt of satisfaction. The sound, growling from deep in his chest, brought back that strange feeling of shameful pride that I had started to become so familiar with.

"Now look at me," he said in the voice of authority. The mere sound of the words brought a clench between my thighs even as I obeyed, and I looked up to see a sort of ironic smile on my sponsor's lips. I felt sure—as I if I had begun to read his mind somehow—that the smile meant that the voice had just slipped out.

Mr. Thring hadn't meant to use the overwhelming tool of dominance that Selecta had given him, but his need and his pleasure inside my mouth, and above all his natural dominance had forced it from him. The surprising idea seized me that my master—I realized now that I wouldn't be able to stop thinking of him that way, not with the need between my legs—had in his own heart a kind of compulsion to take charge of my body for his enjoyment. My eyes went wide as I looked at him, the heat surging in my cheeks yet again.

"Put your hand under your nightgown," he said, still using the voice. Once more, I thought I could read his mind in the way his smile broadened slightly. He meant to use it this time, but he meant it ironically. He *knew*. He knew how it turned me on almost unbearably, to be *made* to do all the shameful things I needed.

A thrill of fear made my heart race for a moment. He wouldn't make me say *that*, would he? Could he use the voice of authority to make me admit I paradoxically needed to consent to having my consent taken away? Even as I obeyed him, for I couldn't do otherwise, and thrust my hand down there, the movement of my fingers toward my pussy stopped. I had intended to touch myself, of course, taking his command as permission, but instead I obeyed his words literally, and just rested my hand under the lacy hem, on my hip. The thought that he might force me literally to give up my freedom had chilled me down there.

"You may touch your little cunt," Mr. Thring murmured.

I gasped at the crudity, the terrible degradation, and I did it... started to do it... the naughtiest thing... I found myself, down there... I found the bareness of my shaved pussy, shaved for my sponsor, ready for him, whenever he wanted to... to fuck me. So shamefully wet, so helplessly ready to take the cock he had thrust into my mouth... and with that huge, hard manhood moving inside my mouth, using me for my master's pleasure, I came almost instantly.

My fingers wouldn't stop, though. I needed so much now... He had given me permission, and I had to do it, had to show him that my cunt belonged to him, because he had bought it for his personal use.

Only then, after I had already come once, and my second orgasm had started to build under my frantic, slippery fingertips, did I realize that he hadn't used the voice. Much, much worse... he hadn't even given me an order. He had just given me permission to play with my pussy, my... my... I realized that I had framed the terrible word in my *own* mind too, and that it had turned me on much too urgently.

My cunt. I'm playing with my little cunt while I suck a huge cock. While a wealthy, older man's hardness thrusts in and out of my mouth, and my jaw aches and I nearly gag at every moment of this degrading face-fucking my sponsor is giving me.

And... and he *didn't* order me to do that.

What he *had* ordered me to do... to look at him... *that* would have been nearly impossible, I thought, without the voice. I looked into his eyes, and I saw both lust and a kind of tender fascination. With a rush of exhilaration that sent my pussy spasming into another orgasm, I understood that that emotion, this eye contact, represented the beginning of love.

Love of a kind I had never imagined, in a situation I would never have dreamt might contain the slightest tenderness.

 *sabella*

I felt the warmth in Mr. Thring's lustful smile through my whole body, and it drove away the last remnants of the chill my overthinking about consent had brought down between my thighs. I saw in his eyes that he understood… he *did* understand what I needed. He would never make me literally give up my freedom, as much as I might actually fantasize about being utterly at his mercy.

And he wanted *me*, not just the sexy new body into which Selecta had started to transform my physical shape. I felt my breathing speed up around his thrusting hardness as the thought rose and turned itself over in my mind.

No, this billionaire would never have looked twice at me before I had made the impulsive decision to sign up for this shameful treatment as a Selecta product. But what made him want to dress me in this naughty nightgown with the satin bow across my newly big breasts… what made him want to whip me when I disobeyed him… that lay not in my growing breasts and my burgeoning curves but in my feelings about them, and the man who had paid so much money to command them.

With a sob, my mouth much too full of my sponsor's cock, I tried to relax my jaw and my throat, to provide him with a soft place to enjoy, and I started to come again. My fingers flashed between my thighs, frantically pleasuring my needy clit.

Mr. Thring put his hand on the back of my head and for a moment a thrill of fear went through my whole body as I felt his fingers twine in my hair. I thought he would force his hardness further than I could take it, but at first, he used the hand to guide me gently, and then he held my head still while he showed me I could take him deeper.

"Good girl," he said. He spoke in the voice of authority, then: "Now watch."

I gasped, my mouth hanging open, as he pulled his rigid penis from my mouth and pumped it in his left hand. His own breathing had grown ragged, but the look of dominance on his face spoke of the utter control he exercised over himself. His right hand reached out, to touch my jaw with his fingertips, softly, just reminding me of how I had served him so wantonly on my knees.

My forehead creased hard as I watched my sponsor show me how he liked his manhood treated, the slow strokes and then the fast ones. I found I could look into his eyes, too—that his command to watch meant to me that I could watch all of him. I saw him gazing down at me, and I saw the need to possess me growing so strong in his eyes that with a sob I came again.

Just as my body jerked with that new climax, I saw Mr. Thring's hips move in a similar, though much more forceful way. My eyes widened as he gave a grunt from deep in his chest, and then I cried out in shameful surprise as his seed spurted from his cock and landed on my chin, and then, as he had promised, the pretty satin bow that made my big new breasts a present for him to unwrap when he chose.

His semen felt warm on my skin. My sponsor's smile to see me wearing his sperm, to have the essence of his desire and his use of me on my face and my silky night-gown sent a wave of shame through me, so that I stopped my fingers' movement between my legs and pulled my hand out from beneath the nightgown.

"Good girl," he said again. "That felt great."

I bit my lip as I looked up at him, remembering the command to watch and unable to disobey it even now that he had come on me and I wanted desperately to hide my semen-stained face.

"You may stand up," he said, reaching down to help me to my feet. I closed my eyes because the permission to rise seemed to take the place of the previous instruction, though I didn't feel entirely certain of it until I felt his arms enfold me.

The hug erased every earlier order. I felt that assurance from my sponsor flow through my body, somehow, without his saying a thing. Moreover, his strong arms, with one hand on the back of my head and the other on my bottom under the nightgown, told me of the tenderness within his lust. His embrace dominated me; my sponsor hugged me, and for a long moment I didn't hug him back but only surrendered to his arms.

Then the warmth of his body, both literal and emotional, seemed to burst into my own limbs, and I put my own arms around him and clung to him. A little whimper came from my throat. Inside me—in my chest and my belly, my hips and my bottom, and above all between my thighs—that hug, the perfect force of it, not too hard and not too soft, seemed to awaken all the strange emotions and ideas of the strangest day of my life.

Somewhere in my mind I felt certain I could feel Selecta's booth or their pill continuing its work—accelerating its work—in me. The fiercely independent part of me tried to get the rest of my brain to despise Mr. Thring's embrace for that reason.

It felt much, much too good for such a scornful dismissal, though. I could feel the changes in my body, the way my big breasts pushed against his hard chest and my heart-shaped ass seemed to mold itself to his fondling hand. More importantly, though, I could feel how for the first time sex—hot, shameful sex—and affection had actually come together inside me, and the comforting embrace of the wealthy, older man who had just used me for his pleasure made me feel valued and safe.

"Thank you, Isabella," he said. "I'll see you tomorrow evening."

"Tomorrow?" I whispered into the fabric of his suit coat. My mouth felt strange, speaking after having my sponsor's hardness thrusting so urgently and arrogantly between my lips. My sudden alarm at being parted from the man who had done that to me took me by surprise.

"Yes," he said. "It's all on a schedule."

"Schedule," I repeated, my brow furrowing. Then I couldn't help whispering, "What happens next?"

"You know what happens next, my dear," he replied, his deep voice making my own body vibrate. "Before I come back, they're going to get you ready for me."

My lips parted and my breathing sped up yet again.

"Ready for what?" I asked, fearing the answer as much as I needed it.

"For fucking, Isabella," he growled. "When I come back, I'm going to fuck you the way you deserve."

That evening Maria took me to the gym for a walk on the treadmill and then to the dining room for a delicious salmon dinner—good protein, she said, to help build my new body. The tablet Selecta had given me chimed from the bedside table right at 9pm, which Maria had told me was lights out for me so that I could get proper sleep. On the tablet I found a message from Carl.

Dear Isabella, the mail read.

Thank you again for being such a good girl for me earlier today. I just want you to know that I'm very happy you're considering accepting me as a sponsor.

Yours, Carl

I went to sleep that night thinking about him, of course. My tongue, moving in my mouth, reminded me of how it had felt to have a wealthy man's hard penis in there, using me for his enjoyment. My hand had found its way under the waistband of my panties before I remembered that Maria had told me I wasn't allowed to play with myself. My face went hot as I pulled my hand up. They might not be watching on their cameras at the moment, but I remembered the sensor down there and thought about what it might show Dr. Hethcote about the state of my pussy.

Carl. The name didn't seem any less dominant than *Mr. Thring.*

My fingers had ended up on my tummy, which I realized felt much tauter than it had that morning, despite also seeming to have swelled out just a little to complement my broadening hips. I couldn't help stroking myself there, as in the dark my forehead creased with the need that felt so much more urgent than it had ever felt before.

The need for... for... I felt myself drifting off, and I thanked God that Selecta had at least exhausted my body enough to allow me some rest.

I awoke, though, with the next words in my mind: *the need for sex*. Down there, inside my panties. *For fucking.* My sleepy hand found its way downward again. I put it between my thighs, outside my panties. I bit my lip at the dampness I found.

I moved my hips, my half-awake brain somehow deciding that if I did that and rubbed myself against my fingers instead of using them inside my underwear, I wouldn't break a rule. I heard a whimper come from my throat, but I convinced myself somehow that some other naughty girl had made it.

"Isabella," said Maria's voice from the tablet on the bedside table, her voice brusque and, I thought, a little annoyed, "go ahead and get out of bed. There are instructions on the screen for how to get ready in the bathroom this morning."

My cheeks blazing, I yanked my hand from between my legs and sat up in bed. I grabbed the tablet to distract myself. What I found didn't help.

Good morning, Isabella. The following is the beginning of the protocol for your morning ablutions, which is an essential part of your treatment.

Start by removing your sleepwear. Do not urinate. You are to look at yourself in the bathroom mirror. You will receive instructions from the speaker in the bathroom, and when you comply with them you will be permitted to go to the toilet and relieve yourself.

I felt hot all over as I rose from the bed and went into the big pink bathroom. I stripped off my t-shirt and panties, and with my jaw set defiantly I turned to the mirror over the sink.

I couldn't suppress a gasp at what I saw. Yes, it was me, but my body... my full breasts... my broad hips. It hadn't been a dream or anything like it. I had started to turn into a... a... *bombshell.* It seemed the only word that worked.

The memory of the look in Carl's eyes as he had fucked my face, and the way he had whipped me, the way he had hugged me after he had come on me, came flooding into my mind. Shame and pride—vanity, even—seemed to compete inside me at the mental images and the reflection before me in the glass. My sponsor found this body irresistible... so irresistible that he had paid God only knew how much money and would keep paying for the privilege of possessing me... of fucking me.

Maria's voice echoed off the tile. I looked up above the mirror and saw a small grille that obviously covered the speaker.

"Isabella, I'm going to start the next part of the protocol now. It's important that you follow the instructions you'll hear, though I know they'll probably be a little embarrassing. If you refuse to do as you're told, there will be consequences as outlined in the agreement you signed."

"Consequences?" I asked, looking up at the speaker so I didn't have to see my blush in the mirror. My mouth twisted to the side as my bladder let me know I needed to get whatever this was over with as soon as possible.

"A trip to the discipline room," she said flatly, "with your prospective sponsor this time."

My lips parted as I began to frame an outraged objection, but the voice—the one from the booth, the one that resembled Carl's—came out of the speaker before I could utter a syllable.

"Hold your breasts in your hands, Isabella," it said. "Weigh them. Present them to yourself in the mirror."

CHAPTER 19

 arl

I watched the bathroom scene on Isabella's video feed. When Selecta had mailed me to ask if I'd like to see it, at first, I had mixed feelings. I didn't think of myself as the kinkiest of guys—dominant, yes, so I never denied an interest in BDSM as part of my ethos of traditional gender-roles. Nor did I think anything that happened between consenting adults in the bedroom, the bathroom, or anywhere else could be morally wrong.

I suppose I just hadn't really considered all the possibilities for sexual discipline, and so I didn't have an immediately positive reaction to the news that part of Isabella's therapy would happen in the bathroom. Or, to put it more directly, my cock didn't leap to attention at the thought.

The email, however, had proven quite persuasive.

You may be surprised to learn that our scientists consider these bathroom sessions an essential part of a girl's therapy. A submissive woman's ingrained and generally only semiconscious thoughts and feelings about not only the toilet but also the shower, the bathtub, and even the mirror where she checks her appearance multiple times a day after urinating are nearly always much stronger than most observers, even astute ones, would imagine.

Very importantly, because these ideas are for the most part semiconscious, she herself hardly understands how important the bathroom is in the makeup of her submissive sexuality. Moreover, the very nature of her bathroom-related sexual feelings, especially concerning relieving herself on the toilet, makes them the object of repression so intense that one of our chief researchers has gone so far as to publish on "The Bathroom as Repression Engine."

What does this mean to you, Carl, and to Isabella?

I couldn't help smiling as I read, at the clever personalization. Selecta's marketing department contained just as much talent as the rest of the megacorp. Now that they had their hooks into me for several million dollars, much of it nonrefundable, they had no intention of letting me off the line.

Not that I had any desire to wriggle free at this point. Ten minutes before I had received this email, I had just increased the *Selecta Arrangements* line-item in my budget spreadsheet by ten million dollars.

Well, to cut through what can seem like scientific mumbo jumbo, our doctors think there may well be no better place to help a woman learn to submit happily to her sponsor than the bathroom. What you'll see if you tune into Isabella's bathroom session tomorrow morning is a young woman experiencing the connection between shame and arousal in her psyche more intensely than she ever imagined she could.

From this point on, Isabella will not be allowed to climax until you permit it, when you have vaginal intercourse with her for the first time tomorrow evening. After this bathroom session, as you'll see if you watch, she will be desperate to orgasm. That's the precise state necessary to complete her physical transformation. You may even see her breasts get bigger, her hips widen, and her backside grow more luscious right there in the bathroom.

It's also, coincidentally enough, the perfect state for her to provide you with the pleasure you deserve as her sponsor and a member of the SA Platinum Program. When you fuck Isabella tomorrow—whether or not you tune in to her bathroom session, of course—she will be ready to respond just as submissively as she should.

I didn't have a raging erection, certainly, by the time I had finished reading it. The stirrings down there, however, had grown enough in magnitude that I put an alarm in my calendar for 7am—*Watch I.*

Isabella

. . .

I wanted to close my eyes and I wanted to keep them open. The sight of my naked self, me but also not me, holding my big breasts up as if I was presenting them to my master, made me feel faint.

"Think about what your husband..."

Oh, goddammit. How could *that* word... a word that shouldn't really have anything sexual about it, because it meant, you know, hearth and home and...

And a firm hand.

My hips jerked as my pussy clenched.

At the fucking word husband. *For fuck's sake.*

Not my sponsor. The voice had said *husband.*

"... would like to do with breasts like those."

I felt them grow. I literally felt a little tremor under my fingers inside my breasts. Something about the way my arousal—*this* kind of arousal, the tiny but burgeoning fantasy about having a man to watch over me, a husband with a firm hand applied regularly to my bare bottom—interacted with whatever drugs they had given me.

Who knew whether the pill had just been some kind of placebo, and the real drugs were in the food? Or the air in my bedroom? It didn't even matter, because I literally had just felt my breasts grow bigger, even if in the mirror the change might have been small enough that my eyes

175

couldn't detect it. It wasn't cartoonish, but that subtlety made it all the more powerful between my thighs and in the instant stiffening of the quarter-sized brown nipples on my... my *tits*.

What would Carl... my sponsor... my *husband*... want to do with those big tits?

I had no idea where the kinky image came from. I had no memory of seeing some porn video out of the corner of my eye or overhearing a raunchy conversation between coworkers that featured the picture that rose into my mind and made me bite my lower lip and whimper. I definitely had never intentionally read anything or seen anything that had shown me what I instantly understood to be the thing submissive women lucky enough to have big tits could do for their masters—or submissive wives for their husbands, their cheeks burning just as hot as mine did now.

Maybe I came up with it all on my own in that moment, out of my own imagination, freed by Selecta after so many years of pushing down such imaginings under the veil of modesty and decency. If so, I knew even as I invented it for myself that it must be a thing men like Carl knew how to demand and thus—in the case of a girl like me, with needs like mine—get when he chose to demand it.

I saw it in the mirror, like an overlay atop the already lewd reflection of a desperately needy young woman offering her tits to anyone who wanted to use her. In my mind's eye, I saw Carl's huge, hard cock sliding between my big breasts, in the soft valley there. I heard his noises of satisfaction and pleasure—I knew them already, didn't I, from the way he had used my mouth yesterday?

Husband. Surely, they wouldn't lead a girl on like that? Had he... had he *said* something, or...

I just met him yesterday. How can I be thinking about this? About him marrying *me?*

Marrying me, and on my wedding night this new body would feel like my new husband were taking my virginity, wouldn't it? And the things Carl, my sponsor, my master, my husband would demand of me...

I gasped, looking at myself, holding my breasts, showing them off, presenting them. I panted with need as I felt the ache down there, where he had promised to fuck me.

But first he'll use these tits, won't he? He wants to get the most out of this body he's bought for me.

My right hand moved of its own accord: I definitely didn't intend it to go down between my thighs that way. It just happened, and then the voice spoke again.

"Stop, Isabella. Don't be naughty."

I snatched my hand away, but then I had to put it back a microsecond later because the fullness of my bladder, from which the terrible urgency of my arousal had distracted me for the last few minutes, suddenly became much, much too present in my mind. The burning in my cheeks, which had begun the moment the voice had told me to offer my breasts and grown hotter when it had invited me to think about my husband enjoying my tits, became an inferno as I had to press my fingers down low between my legs to keep myself from peeing onto the pink tile.

My face went from a needy pout to a desperate mask of mortified, beseeching woe. My eyes sought the toilet, and my body turned toward it, my right foot taking a step in that direction.

"Isabella," the voice said. "Did I give you permission to use the potty?"

No no no no no. My mind pleaded with me to resist. It wasn't the voice of authority, Carl's special way to enforce my actions, and besides, I thought, even if it had been, surely, I wouldn't have obeyed? This... this submission thing didn't apply to stuff where I really didn't want to comply, and I absolutely, positively wanted to go to the toilet and release what felt like a gallon of pee in my bladder.

The word *potty* seemed with its crushing degradation to make my need to let go so much worse that I let out a wrenching, beseeching sob.

"Please?" I begged, looking up at the speaker. Then, because I felt my pee starting, despite all the kegels I had done from the first time I read some other associate member's advice on the SA forum to do thirty of them every day, I humiliated myself even more. "Please, may I go?"

Like a little girl—just like a little girl.

Oh no. That thought... I hadn't had any idea when I had let it come into my mind practically unawares, how terribly powerful it would be for me. A little girl in need of a firm hand because she liked to touch her new body. The pressure of my fingers atop my pussy suddenly became dismayingly ambiguous. To my horror—but also to my helpless pleasure, I felt an instant orgasm coming on, the kind I had only too recently realized I was capable of.

"Go ahead, Isabella," the voice said. "But do not allow yourself to orgasm. You will climax when your sponsor permits it."

I darted toward the toilet. I whimpered as I felt how the pee started to dampen my pussy even before I could sit, but then, letting out a cry of discomfort and relief and needy pleasure, I released the stream at last. The cry became a sob because the need had grown so great and the pleasure made me want to put my hand down there, shameful as it would be, and play with myself while the golden stream gushed into the bowl.

"Good girl," said the voice.

"Oh God," I whispered, closing my eyes and scrunching up my face. I tried to concentrate on the feeling of my knees in the palms of my hands, my fingers stroking the tops of my shins. The idea of being a good girl for peeing on the potty, the swell of silly pride and abject shame... and unwelcome arousal at the sheer sensation of letting go and feeling the stream, warm and wet and so embarrassing... I couldn't keep it out.

At last the flow eased and the last few drops trickled into the bowl. I turned to look for the toilet paper, but I saw to my dismay that it was on the other side of the... the other thing.

Bidet. I had recalled the word with difficulty the day before, and now the very sight of it brought heat to my cheeks.

"You may go to the bidet, Isabella," the voice told me. "It's automatic: it will turn on once you're squatting over it."

Why should a device that was intended simply to clean a part of the body that needed special attention make my face blaze this way? Why should it make my nipples stiff as I contemplated squatting that way, cleansing my pussy the way French women did?

French women... French girls... French... whores. Like the fantasy of my sponsor's huge, hard penis between my breasts, the thought seemed to come from something I had read or seen but didn't remember at all. Except that its most shameful part had stuck, somehow, in my mind.

Am I a little girl? Do little girls use a bidet? No... French whores use a bidet to get their cunts clean for the men who use them.

The thought brought a spasm of need down there, so great that I gasped as my bottom squirmed on the toilet seat. I rose, desperate to cover it over, and I moved toward the strange porcelain bowl with the silver fixtures in it.

CHAPTER 20

sabella

I willed myself to turn and squat, trying to pretend the bidet represented nothing but a weirdly low sink. I knew from a friend who had traveled in Europe that French people—and not only the French, but lots of Europeans—didn't think of them as anything special. Indeed, my friend had said that in Europe they thought *we* were weird for *not* cleaning up that way after using the toilet.

That thought made me realize, though, with a little grimace, just how connected the bathroom must be in my mind and even in my body with shame and modesty and... submission. The closer I got to straddling the thing, the hotter my face became. The posture seemed degrading in itself because the voice had told me to do it.

I couldn't shove it away as I complied, as I put my feet on either side of the bowl and bent my knees to expose my most private places to the stream of warm water that sprang up from the silver fountain. The idea, the fantasy that went beyond the factual, utilitarian nature of the bidet... how a man like Carl might tell a girl... a French girl or... or an American girl like me, dressed in a sexy nightgown like the one he had stained with his semen... tell me with the voice of authority so that I couldn't refuse... tell me to straddle the strange bowl whose purpose was so cryptic at first, so hidden to the innocent and modest but so obvious and lewd to the initiated... tell me to get myself ready... tell me to get my pussy... no, my *cunt*... my cunt and... my whole upper body seemed to blaze with mortified heart... and my anus...

"Put your hand down there now, Isabella," the voice said. "Your sponsor wants your vagina and your anus clean and ready for his penis."

Ready for fucking. Carl wants me ready for fucking.

"Oh God," I moaned as I put my hand down there and added more pleasure to the seductive, soothing feeling of the water. I hadn't imagined something so... so... dirty could feel so good.

I almost giggled at that thought, because really, of course, dirty things were dirty, a lot of the time, because they felt so good, weren't they.

"Remember, you must not climax, Isabella," warned the voice.

My hand froze between my legs, but I had to close my eyes to see the vivid image that seemed to leap into my mind's eye, of what would happen if the sensor between my thighs, right where I had my soothing fingers now, showed an orgasm. How they would tell Carl... how angry he would be... how he would take me to the discipline room...

I gasped because my fingers had started to move again of their own accord. My other hand had risen to squeeze my breast... my enormous boob and pinch the nipple.

The paddle... the wooden paddle I had seen on the rack... the kind of paddle a strict husband kept hanging somewhere just out of sight... in the pantry, maybe... the family paddle, used to keep a man's wife in the proper fear of her lord and master...

"Isabella," said Maria, opening the bathroom door unceremoniously. "Get up and come here. Put your hands on your head. You're clean enough down there. There's a gift from your sponsor waiting for you."

Trying hard to keep the pout of humiliated arousal from becoming any deeper on my forehead and my cheeks than it already was, I complied. For a moment, I looked at the tiled floor, feeling unable to meet Maria's eyes, but then a wave of resentment and anger seemed to rise from the soles of my feet on that cool, smooth surface and I lifted my gaze to meet hers.

Maria looked back at me calmly and ironically, and I felt the heat rush yet again to my cheeks, my brow, and all the way to the roots of my hair. At least it was a different kind of display, a different kind of heat, though.

I knew it as a very sulky, even peevish, kind of emotion, but I welcomed it all the same because it drove the apparently endless wanton need from the troublesome region between my waist and my knees. It thankfully made me forget about my breasts, their new heaviness, and their stiff, tingly nipples.

"Can I put my hands down now?" I demanded, putting as much disdain in my voice as I could. Who was Maria to give me orders? Who was Selecta, even, to pretend that this... this *therapy*... had anything in it intended to help *me*? Fine, I had stupidly signed an agreement for what they had described as a second chance at the dream of romance, and I had ended up as some kind of medically-enhanced prostitute, but they kept acting like I should be grateful to follow their utterly degrading protocols.

"I don't know," Maria answered. "Can you put them down without playing with yourself, Isabella? When you see what your sponsor has given you, will you be able to keep your hands away from your vulva?"

My face tried to put on a look that reflected the completely unwelcome thrill of arousal that shot through me. My upper teeth moved to bite my lower lip. I stopped the expression in mid-bite and turned it into a snort of derision.

Vulva. I hated that word almost as much as *cunt.* No... more. The doctor's word, the word that seemed the most clinical, supercilious way to talk about a woman's pussy. My mind almost went down that path—almost discovered the memory, the recollected sound, of Carl saying "cunt," almost realized that I didn't hate the word *cunt* at all now, and that the word *vulva* apparently could turn me on in a mortifying fashion too.

Again my forehead tried to crease, but I worked my face into a sneer instead.

"Sure," I told the nurse.

"Go ahead," Maria said. "But remember it's your sponsor who will take you to the discipline room at this point if you disobey your caregivers' instructions."

As I lowered my hands, my mouth twisting to the side with the effort to keep my face looking as resentful as I could manage, I wondered for a split second about Maria's calm tone. Was she actually trying to turn me on under that placid, clinical cover?

I walked quickly by her, wanting to get what I felt sure would be an embarrassing revelation over with. Another babydoll nightgown, I felt certain—this one see-through, maybe.

The box lay open on my bed; inside, a note on his expensive stationery sat atop it. I shook my head when I saw what the white cardboard rectangle held, under that note. My hands... *fuck you, Maria...* I clenched them into fists: I couldn't help it.

I stepped to the bed, my head still shaking.

Dear Isabella, I can't wait to see you. I'll be there at noon, and I'll take you to the dining room wearing your presents. We'll have lunch, and then we'll come back to your room. I'll take my time making you mine, I promise, and we'll discuss our arrangement before I enjoy you. By the time I leave, though, you will belong to me if I believe I have it in my power to make you happy. I hope this gift helps you get yourself into the proper frame of mind. Affectionately, Carl

He knocked on my door at 12:02. I had been ready since 11:55, just sitting on the bed wearing the... the things. I didn't even know what to call them... well, *it*—the other things were more familiar, even if I hadn't ever worn this *kind* of panties, stockings, or even shoes. I refused to look at myself in the mirror. The slightly scratchy feeling of all that lace against my skin, holding me *in* and holding me *up* in my most sensitive places... it already seemed enough to make me do something foolish. Whether that foolishness would come in the form of trying to escape from the underground R&D facility or putting my hand inside the lacy white thong as I watched myself do the naughty, disobedient thing, I didn't even want to think about.

The knock came at last and I stood up, and Carl opened the door before I could even start toward it, the way the doctors and the nurses did, just coming into the room to deliver the treatment I needed whether I thought I needed it or not. He wore a navy blue suit today rather than a dark grey one, but he looked just as devastatingly handsome, his beard just as neatly trimmed.

In his chocolate eyes I saw what I must look like—not in any reflection but in the way the corners crinkled with an instant smile that somehow seemed both happy and hungry. Wolfish, even. So avid that it made me shiver and sent a hot flush to my cheeks. His hunger had me as its object and that forced me to see myself in the lingerie he had dressed me in.

Carl made it absolutely clear too, that he wanted me to see myself that way. He crossed the distance to me as I took a little step back, my hands in front of me in sudden alarm. He reached his right hand out and curved it around the small of my back, right where the strange, stiff, satiny fabric of the bustier, or basque, or merry widow, or whatever it was left off and my bare skin began. He took hold of me there, and he turned me toward the vanity and propelled me toward it, so that I understood even before he spoke exactly what he intended.

"Look at yourself," he said, using the voice of authority to make absolutely certain I would obey.

The first thing I saw was my face and the humiliating, needy pout of my lips that had come onto my features the moment he had started to move toward me and had grown to mortifying proportions when he touched me and turned me.

Then I saw his face behind me, above me, and I became instantly conscious of the disobedience that represented. He had told me to look at myself, and he had used the voice, and I could only behold those narrowed eyes, that hungry smile for an instant before I must lower my gaze. I couldn't defy my sponsor, as frightened as he made me with his all-too-clear intent to possess me in ways no man had ever possessed me before.

He lowered his hand as I lowered my eyes. He took hold of my bottom, as if to tell me what would happen to me if I disobeyed. He squeezed the taut flesh of my now full, heart-shaped ass and reminded me of how he had used his belt yesterday to keep me in line. His middle finger found the thin, lacy strap of the thong between my cheeks and stroked it to make sure I remembered all his intentions for me.

With a tiny whimper, I looked at myself fully for the first time in the impossibly sexy white lingerie.

Whatever the garment around my waist and under my breasts, the cups just barely covering my nipples, might be called, it emphasized my new curves so strongly that I couldn't suppress a gasp. I didn't think it was a corset because I knew corsets restricted and cinched. Thanks to Selecta, I didn't have any need of cinching. My bare waist below the bustier looked stunningly slim, my hips alluringly wide with the tiny lacy thong setting them off to perfection.

The mesh of the thong's front panel showed the viewer that I had no hair there and the virginal white seemed to tell a lewd tale of wedding-night innocence, of a bride prepared for her dominant groom. I thought of the bidet and bit my lip... a French whore, or a pampered bride... either way bought and paid for and made to ready her most private places for the man who owned her.

CHAPTER 21

 sabella

"You look gorgeous this way, my dear," Carl murmured into my ear. "I think I need to give you a little appetizer before we go for lunch."

My lips parted; I watched them part. I saw the alarm, the shame, the arousal all come into my face at the same time, because I understood what he must mean despite the vagueness of his words. And I knew that I could only understand the words that way because I *needed* them to mean the filthy, degrading thing my sponsor must intend to say.

My cheeks had gone crimson.

"I... I... I mean... wh-what..." The stammering, the rapid breathing... the mortification swelled in my chest as I heard myself trying to pretend that I didn't know the answer—that it hadn't caused a jerk of my hips and a clench of my pussy inside the lacy white thong.

"Shh, Isabella," he said. I thought he might explain, just to be crude, just to make me blush even harder and to enjoy the sight of my offended modesty. Or perhaps, I supposed, he might make another innuendo. Instead, he used the voice of authority, and an irresistible thrill of vanity prickled the back of my neck as I understood his urgency could only come from how thoroughly I must have aroused him.

How hard his cock must have gotten, just looking at me and fondling my ass.

"Get on the bed," he said in that lower tone that I felt now I knew much, much too well. "On your back."

He squeezed my bottom—*my sweet ass*, I couldn't help thinking with another rush of shameful pride—one more time, and then he used his hold there to start to turn me around to the bed.

I realized that the way the voice of authority must work in my head was that one command replaced another. Whatever subconscious mechanism Selecta had installed or activated in my nervous system would release me from whatever Carl had commanded the last time he used the voice as soon as he issued new instructions. I complied with his urging hand on my bottom and his arrogant words, feeling my face crumple with humiliation and unwelcome arousal as I turned and moved toward the bed.

Carl kept his hand on my ass as I obeyed him, walking behind me until my knees touched the comforter and, feeling like a sex robot or—*oh God*—an obedient whore, I started to clamber atop the mattress. I heard him kick off his shoes.

I had known from the moment he said *appetizer* that he would use my mouth again in some way, but I didn't understand why he had told me to lie on my back on the bed. My mind filled with different pictures, and for the first time since arriving in this strange scientific bordello I found that the lewdness of my subconscious had no ready answer. The removal of Carl's shoes, though, must mean that he meant to get onto the bed with me. The thought brought a whimper to my lips as I turned on all fours on the bed to see him looming over me, tall and handsome and with such hunger in his eyes that the whimper became a little sob of fear and need.

I trembled as I kept turning and lowering myself to follow my sponsor's instructions. I couldn't keep my eyes off him and the way he looked at me, so satisfied and yet at the same time so avid. He had bought himself a precious thing, and he was happy—*no*, I thought with another vain thrill, *overjoyed*—with his purchase. He wanted very badly, though, to use his treasure… to see what I might be good for, how much pleasure he could find in me.

Then I had turned all the way over and looking up at his tall, muscular frame, so elegantly dressed in the business suit, I saw him reach for me. I cried out, and I couldn't have said in that moment what the emotion was in that cry—all of them, most likely: fear and need, of course—but *hope* too... and I suddenly didn't want to deny it, *love* even... or maybe just its beginnings. Some feeling, though, of unmistakable warmth, not just between my thighs and in my cheeks, but in my heart too.

I had no idea how the alarming, dominant, *aggressive* way Carl reached his hands toward me, the right one toward my pussy and the left one toward my breasts, could make me feel the stirrings of love for him. My incomprehension didn't matter, though—didn't even come close to mattering. I could blame Selecta and their pills and their booth and their voice, but I knew deep down that just as with the voice of authority, they had only uncovered something inside me that I might never have had the ability to acknowledge out loud.

Even if I couldn't admit it now and might never be able to admit it even to Carl, I could most certainly feel it, how his sheer, masterful aggressiveness toward my body affected me. How my sponsor's effortless assertion of his masculine rights... to order me onto the bed... to put out his hands and simply take hold of my most intimate places and seize them, much more for his pleasure than for mine... how it didn't only make my pussy clench and my wet need gush into my panties but also made me want to hold him and have him hold me, and to fall asleep in his arms, night after night forever.

His fingers reached inside the huge cups of the bustier and found my left nipple. He pinched it hard, even as his right hand went between my thighs, his middle fingers working up inside the gusset of the tiny panties. My body bucked on the bed, and I wanted Carl Thring more than I had ever imagined I could want a man—more than I had ever wanted anything in my life.

The tips of his two middle digits plunged inside me to find my need and to spread it expertly upwards. My back arched and my hips pushed against his hand, desperate to take in more of that rough, probing touch. Heat surged above and below as I realized how wet I must be, if that forced entry, that firm rubbing felt so terribly good.

"You're a little whore, aren't you?" Carl murmured, looking into my eyes. "You need it very, very badly, don't you, Isabella?"

The sobs of wanton arousal that broke from my chest seemed to expand my whole body. It shook my breasts in Carl's hand as he moved it from right to left, freeing both of those enormous tits from the cups of the bustier.

"Answer me," he said, his eyes narrowing.

No, he didn't use the voice, I realized. I could refuse. I *did* refuse. I shook my head, my hair threshing on the pillow, my face a mask of lewd woe. I pursed my lips firmly as if I knew—for of course I did know—what it would mean, so very soon now, to open my mouth to my sponsor. A moment before I hadn't understood, but Carl had brought his left hand down to his waist to unzip his fly, and my too-active imagination had painted the whole scene of what he meant to do.

He smiled and his right hand left my pussy. I mewed in protest through my tightly closed lips, but he held up his forefinger in front of my face and wagged it so I could see the sheen from my wetness glinting in the light from the room's recessed fixtures.

"If you don't need it, my dear," he said, with such mocking arrogance that I couldn't help gasping, "why should I give it to you, even with my fingers?"

"Oh... oh God," I whispered as my bottom squirmed with the desire I couldn't, it seemed, ever voluntarily confess. I had felt certain he would use the voice because to my dismay, I knew how badly I *did* want to tell him—how much I wanted his fingers, his cock, *him*.

I knew suddenly that he wouldn't, though, or at least not until he had thoroughly demonstrated how easily he could master me without it. He had his hardness in his hand, and it jutted from the front of his trousers like a thick tree branch. I looked in helpless, obscene fascination... at its length, its rigidity.

I need it... I need it so bad.

Without warning he started to get onto the bed, over me —on top of me. I let out a little cry of alarm, suddenly afraid he might put his weight on me. He didn't, though. Having straddled me at my waist, he moved carefully further up, his eyes locked on mine as he enacted precisely the shameful scenario I had pictured a moment before.

The hard penis that had kept my attention rapt from the moment he freed it from his fly came closer. A complicated, fleshy branch, a scepter, veined and throbbing slightly with Carl's pulse. The most sensitive part of his body, even if it seemed so rigid and dominant, so impervious to anything a little whore like me could do.

I felt my eyes widen as I realized I had just thought of myself that way... and I felt the clench it had caused between my thighs.

As if he could read my mind, he murmured, so far above me I almost couldn't make out the words, "My little whore in white."

Just as he said the degrading thing, he reached the place I knew he had meant to go from the moment he had decided that I must have an appetizer before lunch. He laid his hardness between my breasts, his hands on my bare shoulders, caressing the soft skin there—much softer now thanks to Selecta, the megacorp I couldn't help thinking Carl had simply used as a billion-dollar madam to procure my body for his enjoyment.

His hands moved to my breasts, his body straightening above me until he seemed to loom impossibly high over my chest, my face, my widening eyes. He kneaded them gently, pressing the nipples with his thumbs, rubbing them in circles until it felt like they couldn't get any stiffer, any more revealing of his power over me.

"I'm glad you're not a virgin between your thighs, Isabella," he said slowly and, it seemed to me, reflectively. I felt my face crumple at just how great a flush of mortifying pride this sent through my body. "But I'm also glad you have virginities for me to take, nonetheless. I had your mouth yesterday, and I shall have your anus later today."

"Oh..." I sobbed. "No, please."

"Yes, my dear," he said, his rumbling voice seeming to travel through his body, through the strong thighs that surrounded my upper body. "But now I'm going to take a very special virginity, because these lovely breasts are only a day old, aren't they?"

He squeezed them as he spoke, just a little roughly, and I cried out, as much in need as in discomfort.

"Take them in your hands," he told me. "Keep them nice and close together. I'm going to fuck them now."

Yes, by that point I had imagined it, and Carl had done what I imagined. The ultra-dominant straddling of my body, the looming over me, the cock between my newly grown boobs. I hadn't imagined he would make *me* participate that way, or that he would call it fucking. I didn't know why it mattered even, but the way he said it made my hips jerk, my pussy spasm with longing for his skillful fingers.

Nor had he used the voice. Why hadn't he used the voice? If he didn't use the voice, how could I obey him?

But Carl knew precisely how to manage me, I found out then even more thoroughly than I had known it the moment before.

"If you want to come at all today," he said. "You're going to obey me."

arl

The pleasure to be found between a woman's big, soft breasts had always seemed to me one of life's greatest luxuries. Isabella's firm, grapefruit-sized globes, though, exceeded every bit of my aroused anticipation. Much of the nearly overwhelming pleasure that shot through my nervous system and ran like electric joy over my skin must have come from the silken softness of her bosom on its own, but much of it also came from the sweet pout of transgressed innocence on her face as I taught her how to do the naughty thing.

My rock-hard cock slid between those sweet, pillowy tits. I kept my hands on them for a moment longer, squeezing them together around my shaft as I fucked, finding my breathing had grown labored with the pleasure. Then I reached out to caress Isabella's gorgeous face, still moving my hips and sliding my manhood back and forth steadily.

The delight ebbed a little without the pressure that made the valley of her bosom so perfect a place of pleasure. That slight loss was more than compensated by the wideness of Isabella's eyes as she felt my fingertips on her cheek, moving lingeringly down to her slender neck and up to her hairline.

Her body bucked under mine as if she had just physically taken in what I had said about the pleasure she must not expect to receive if she refused to provide it to her sponsor.

"Please," she whispered, and at the same time her hands came up from her sides around my clothed legs and took tentative hold of her breasts. The crease in her forehead deepened and the expression on the lovely face I cradled in my hands grew charmingly puzzled.

"How…" she started, hesitantly pushing the creamy globes together around my penis. She licked her lips, her eyes widening at the sensation of my cock sliding against her sensitive flesh, with her own hands creating the pleasurable constriction for my fucking. "Is this…?"

I let out an involuntary grunt of pleasure, as much at the sweet innocence of her confusion as at the sheer ecstasy my cock felt in that heavenly valley. To my joy, Isabella couldn't suppress the smile that came instantly to her lips as she realized she had made me answer the question without my even intending to.

I smiled back, but the heat of the dominant blood in my veins urged me to master her still more, to make sure my new bed girl understood what it meant to serve a wealthy man. I had dressed her in this elaborate white lingerie, the lacy bustier that set off her stunning body so sexily, the tiny panties that invited a man's eye and showed him more than a good girl should ever show in her underwear, the fishnet stockings that drew the eye down her shapely legs to the heels that made a sponsor's rear view so cock-stiffening.

I moved my hands around and I tightened my grip on her head—not abruptly, but decisively, so that Isabella cried out.

"Open your mouth," I said, "and put out your tongue."

"Oh no," she breathed. "Oh… please."

For the first time, as I heard my Selecta girl respond to my dominance and saw the blush spread over her face, I felt absolutely certain that Isabella had truly benefited from this treatment. In her voice and in her expression, I watched her grasp the full measure of the pleasure she would experience serving me—even in the degrading way that we both needed.

Especially in that degrading way. She gave me a pleading look, and I knew exactly what she wanted and needed most in that moment, more even than the desperate need she so clearly had to come.

I repeated my command, and I used the voice of authority. "Open your mouth and put out your tongue."

* * *

Isabella

I did it. It felt so filthy and scary. Carl rose over me like a skyscraper and his long, rigid penis felt like a burning brand between my breasts. His hands around the back of my head, lifting my face—my mouth above all, for that represented the only part of me he wanted, the part he could use for his humiliating enjoyment.

The head of his cock approaching my open mouth from between my enormous new boobs.

My hands, pressing them together to make a place for fucking.

The tip of his manhood against my tongue, and the sound of my whimper at the feeling. The cock staying there, and my mouth overcome by the urge to kiss and lick—by the faint but mortifying pleasure of sucking the warm thing my sponsor gave me to suck.

Carl let out another one of those grunts of what I thought must be startled pleasure, a sound that could only, I thought, mean that my body had provided more delight than he had expected. He stiffened, and I realized with an eye-widening start that I had brought on his climax. I felt a jet of his hot seed spurt onto my tongue, and I gave my own little cry of surprise, jerking my head back.

He growled deep in this throat, though, a sound like a warning a wolf might give to the cornered prey he means to have for dinner. He held my head in place with his left hand, and he moved his right under my chin.

"Swallow it, girl," he told me, using the voice. "Take it all and swallow it. I promised you an appetizer, didn't I?"

I mewed softly as I obeyed, tasting the strange new flavor, very surprised at how light it was despite its faint bitterness. The heat in my face grew even greater at the swell of pride I found inside me to have done one of the naughtiest things I had ever imagined a girl might do.

"Good girl," Carl murmured, his voice sounding labored as his breath came in short pants that matched the jerking of his hips and the final jets he made me take into my mouth and keep inside me to show how great a gift his "appetizer" represented.

The warm glow that the phrase created inside me had to do with the knowledge that he couldn't refuse me an orgasm now, sure, but it also came from my irresistibly growing affection for him. The embarrassment of needing the filthy things I could no longer deny I needed had given way, or at least started to give way, to gratitude that my sponsor knew how to give them to me.

* * *

Carl didn't bring up anything serious until the waiter put the molten chocolate cake on the table. I blushed a little as I looked at the gorgeous thing, and then a little more as I eagerly put my fork into it ,though it had clearly been put between Carl and me for us to share. As I watched the beautiful liquid chocolate ooze out, I looked up at him and saw him smile warmly back. My embarrassment turned to affection and pure happiness. I smiled back mischievously.

"I still can't believe I can eat this food now," I whispered. I giggled then, probably the first time I had emitted that carefree sound in many months.

My eyes darted up from the plate to Carl's face, just as I put the bite on my fork into my mouth and the glorious warm sweetness, the indescribable flavor of good chocolate lit up my whole body with a feeling so sensual I felt myself squirm in my seat.

I had forgotten through most of the lovely meal about the embarrassing difference in the way my new sponsor and I were dressed: he in the business suit, I in the lacy, ambiguously innocent bustier and thong panties and stockings. Now, as I felt the narrow back of the thong move between my bottom-cheeks and I saw in Carl's eyes his pleasure in looking at a nearly naked girl eating expensive chocolate cake whose beautiful color matched those eyes so perfectly—I became again fully conscious of the lingerie in which he had clad me.

The surge of need and heat that thrilled through my nervous system, shame and arousal intertwined so intricately that I felt like my fingers and toes had become blushing erogenous zones, seemed to radiate from the morsel of cake in my mouth. I gave a little cry of startled ecstasy, and the experience almost became literally orgasmic as the sweetness slid down my throat and I felt Carl's gaze on me, as if he had his hands between my legs, on my bottom, fingers pumping inside me.

"Careful," he said, his eyes blazing, his right hand going out to my left where it rested on the white tablecloth.

For a moment, his voice and his touch only made the problem worse. Despite the lack of any stimulus down there, I squirmed again, and I gasped, feeling my breasts rub against my arms, my ass move over the seat.

"Oh God," I whispered.

"No," Carl said in the voice of authority, and to my astonishment, my body obeyed him, though the pleasure from denying myself release seemed to make the need rise even higher. It made me look at him with such beseeching in my eyes that for a moment I thought he would give in and tell me to climax instead of holding it back.

"You okay?" he asked, smiling like a cat who's just swallowed a tiny bird and knows he'll soon have as many more of them as he wants.

I bit my lip hard and nodded, not sure why I suddenly felt like the man who had just denied me the release I craved and I had become co-conspirators—as if both of us were in pursuit of the greatest possible pleasure, not for him but for both of us.

Carl continued in the same quiet voice, with the same quiet smile then. At first, I couldn't understand what he said, because he had, it seemed to me, changed the subject so entirely.

"I'd like you to move into an apartment I keep very near my own."

I felt myself frown as the words penetrated my mind, my arousal starting to ebb with my momentary confusion. But at the same time, another feeling, an even warmer feeling began to build inside my chest. He hadn't changed the subject, I suddenly understood, and that made the affection rising in my heart all the greater. The near-orgasm with the chocolate cake, of which I took another, less gluttonous and thus a little less orgasmic, bite now in hopes of covering over the power of the emotions affecting me, seemed to melt into an even greater warmth.

"In the same building, actually," he said, the smile on his lips growing rather mischievous. "Well, really, almost next door. Half the penthouse—I live in the other half."

I looked up, because my brain's first response was that he must be joking, while my body's first response involved a strangely visceral feeling of being held, somehow, in Carl's words as if they somehow represented extensions of his strong, embracing arms.

I had to look down when I saw the serious look in my sponsor's eyes.

"Move in," I said softly, looking down at the cake, digging my fork back into it, hardly thinking of the chocolate on the plate while Carl's chocolate eyes remained on my face.

"Yes," he said, not a trace of the mocking irony I had almost expected in his voice. "Hey," he continued, though, "leave some for me."

My eyes darted up to his, but I saw that he had refocused his attention on the cake. I felt him loosen his grip on my hand and I watched with a giggle on my lips as Carl grabbed his own fork and dug it into the middle of the molten cake's beautiful oozy center, pulling away an enormous bite.

I raised my eyes again as he brought the fork to his mouth, and then I had to put both my hands on the table, on either side of my plate, because the sight of my handsome sponsor tasting the sweetness of the cake made me think of his tasting *me*—in the obvious lewd way, of course, with his lips and tongue dominating my pussy, but also in a much more general, holistic, even spiritual way.

I looked down as I felt my brow furrow in arousal, my bottom squirming again in my chair. Then I summoned the courage to look at him again and saw his eyes flare with hunger as he swallowed the last of the cake.

"Would you like to live in a penthouse?" he asked simply.

What else could I do? I nodded, not sure I could even trust my voice to answer in anything other than a croak.

"If you like the penthouse," Carl continued softly and slowly, "do you think you might want to have an even more permanent arrangement?"

 sabella

For a moment I stared at him, literally unable to understand what he had just said. Then I swallowed very hard, and the lingering chocolaty sweetness in my mouth reminded me, like a rhyme that doesn't quite rhyme, of the strange, new taste of his seed. All the remaining blood in my body—it felt like, anyway—went to my face and to my pussy in what seemed like equal measure.

If Carl had meant what I thought he had meant, it didn't represent any kind of marriage proposal I had ever dreamed of. But... had I ever dreamt of becoming a Selecta sugarbaby, as they sometimes called it on the forums? I had never thought of myself that way—had always avoided it, but now when it seemed like the happy ending might be within my reach, it got much harder to resist than it had ever been before.

Would you prefer a little whore with a wet cunt? my brain asked me, *Because that's the way this man thinks of you.*

"Oh God," I breathed. I hadn't taken my eyes from Carl's, and yes, I could see in his eyes that he *did* think of me that way: his little whore with *his* wet cunt. And…

The blood drained from my cheeks and then rushed in like a sudden blaze of daylight and solar heat on a chilly, cloudy day.

And I like it.

I almost asked if he was trying to make fun of me, just to give myself a little time to think. The words died on my lips. I could see in those same lustful, hungry eyes my sponsor's absolute sincerity. I saw that he loved me, too, which shocked me to the core—to the center of my mind and the center of my body—because as strange and even silly as it looked from a logical perspective, I loved him, too.

I loved him even though he gazed at me the way a man looks at his favorite whore.

My husband's little whore.

"Oh my God." The words came out in a little sob, as if some other girl, some other big-breasted little whore with a heart-shaped ass had just responded to a conditional proposal. "Umm…"

I would probably have said, "Okay," and accepted my billionaire's offer of marriage in that ridiculous way if Carl hadn't suddenly stood up and crossed the two-foot distance between our chairs to loom over me. Instead of speaking again, I gasped, looking up at him.

He gave me no time to contemplate what his sudden movement might mean, though an absurd image of him falling to one knee and producing a tiny, velvet-covered box floated into my mind's eye. In the microsecond before Carl carried out his full intention, I rejected that image with the full force of my desperate, wanton need. I might always have *thought* I hoped someday to have a wealthy man on his knees before me, proposing, but Carl Thring should never kneel, and especially not before his little whore.

I'm the one who does the kneeling, I thought with a clench between my legs that made me whimper up into his strong lips surrounded by that soft, beautiful beard as Carl bent down and took my chin into his right hand to tilt it up to him. His left hand went around the back of my head, and I could taste the chocolate of that incredible cake in his mouth yet again.

I wondered if they had put some old-fashioned aphrodisiac in the sponge or the filling or something… Spanish fly, or whatever. But chocolate itself… really good chocolate… didn't it…

Somewhere, a semi-logical voice in my brain noted that I had lost the ability to reason at some point in the last five seconds. My whole world seemed to be my body and

Carl's body, and the astonishing sensations they produced, above all the aching, warm, wetness between my thighs, gushing into the tiny panties in which my... my sponsor? my fiancé? my... master?... had dressed me.

For him. For his pleasure. For his cock.

I cried out into his kissing mouth as I became dimly aware that he had started to move again, raising me up out of the chair and then picking me up off the ground. I heard a clatter behind me, and I realized, even as Carl kept kissing me, that he had somehow, with one arm, cleared the dishes off the table while the other held me aloft without apparent effort.

He laid me down then. On the bare, polished wood on my back, in my bustier and tiny panties and fishnets and heels.

How do these random things... like polished wood...

No, no reason involved... no logic involved. The feeling of smooth, cool wood on my skin and on the stiff satin of the bustier somehow amounted to utter dominance on my master's part and utter submission on mine. His mouth had gone, of course, and my eyes stared up at the white ceiling, the recessed light fixtures.

Dimly, I heard someone enter the room and start to gather the lunch things off the other end of the table where Carl must have shoved them. At the same moment I realized the waiter had begun to do that, I felt Carl take the backs of my knees in his hands and push them toward my breasts, firmly and very far.

211

My huge tits. My knees touched my nipples. I felt the slight roughness of the fishnet mesh, a sensation I had never imagined.

I cried out in shame because the waiter could see, and in abject need because of the way Carl had simply adjusted my body to suit his enjoyment. And the adjustment... no man had ever put me in that posture... no lover had ever even *asked* me to raise my legs like that, to expose all of my most private places that way.

He hadn't even *told* me, not even using the voice of authority. He had just... *done* it.

But he did use the voice then.

"Hold your knees open, Isabella," he said. He spoke much less calmly than he had a moment before, less evenly than on any previous occasion when he had used the voice of authority. I could *hear* his lust. "I'm going to have my real dessert."

"Oh... my..." I couldn't even get the word *God* out of my mouth before my body seemed to turn into the molten center of the chocolate cake. I barely had my knees in my grasp, barely had time to feel the shame and the nearly overwhelming arousal before I felt Carl tug aside the narrow, lacy gusset of the thong and sample the dessert he had just claimed.

The word became a sob... a cry... a long moan. My sponsor knew how to do... how to do...

The very hint of the word—*words*, plural, really... *head... going down... eating out... cunnilingus... cunt-licking...*

They all approached my conscious mind, and they all retreated in the face of the hot shame all over my body as I felt it happening... Carl's consummate skill... the way that despite how me taking him in my mouth seemed absolutely submissive, him tasting me... savoring me... it was undeniably dominant—my master, my *owner*... sampling his property.

He licked up and down, his tongue probing and testing me, somehow... getting me ready... seeing what the cunt he had bought might be good for. He sucked gently at my clit, and I screamed harder and I sobbed.

"So wet, my dear," he murmured. "So needy."

"Oh..." I sobbed. "Oh my..."

The last word still couldn't come out because Carl made my whole body spasm, clench. I clung desperately to my knees as my hips bucked and squirmed as much, more than they would if my sponsor had decided to whip me.

Cunnilingus. The terrible word forced its way into my conscious mind. *He's a master of cunnilingus... as master of little cunts... little whore cunts.*

I couldn't believe I hadn't come yet... I needed the release more badly than I had needed anything in my life. Food and air didn't seem to have a chance when stacked up against the way Carl's lips and tongue made my new body crave the hardness I had come to know so intimately.

His hands spread me open, and I sobbed with the excess of sensation. His fingers went up my thighs and made me terribly conscious of how exposed *all* of me was. When he moved a fingertip to my anus and pressed it inward, it only confirmed that idea with an urgency that brought another whimpering cry to my lips, so submissive that it made my aching sheath clench hard when I heard what I sounded like.

Carl chuckled deep in his chest, and I felt it rumble through his lips into my pussy, so that I whimpered again... clenched again...

"Oh no," I breathed. My climax had come very, very close. "Oh... no..."

Whether he knew I was worried about coming without permission or he actually thought my *no* and the knocking of my shaking head against the wood of the table had to do with where he had put his finger, Carl said, into my pussy so that the warmth of his breath drove me that much closer, "Yes, Isabella. Here, too."

Then I let out a sob of desperation because he rose and stepped away. I had had my eyes closed, but I opened them now to look up at him between my wantonly, shamefully upraised knees.

"Oh my God," I whimpered, realizing that Carl planned to fuck me right here in the dining room. Shame and arousal crescendoed in me—my face, my nipples, my tummy, my pussy and my humiliatingly spread ass.

He had his fly open... he pulled his pants and briefs down to his knees.

"Here, and now," he said, looking into my eyes. "Look at what you did."

I lowered my eyes to where his hardness seemed to flash in his hand, the head of his huge, rigid cock appearing and disappearing in his fist as he pumped himself almost more quickly than I could see with my naked eye.

I let out a sob from deep in my chest, and I seemed at that moment to complete some process of detachment that had started the previous morning when Maria had come into my apartment and started telling me what I had actually signed up for. I had begun then, some new mode of thought seemed now to tell me, to develop an ability to look outside myself and, in fact, *enjoy* my humiliating need for... for this.

All of this. For Carl... for marrying Carl, if Carl wanted to marry me... for submitting to Carl and belonging to Carl.

I could look down at myself—it literally felt that way. I could gaze down from somewhere near the ceiling and look at the impossibly gorgeous, busty, shapely little whore on the table, holding her knees wide for her owner's cock. And at the same time I could look through her eyes... *my* eyes.

I could see Carl's amazing, beautiful, filthy cock... coming closer... closer...

It touched my clit, and my master teased me there so that I sobbed, and the girl on the table cried out, "Please… please… please…" and then the word came out, at last, from my mouth, without any imperative from him. "Master… please, master."

He moved it down, to the entrance… the hole… the sheath for his enormous sword.

"Please, master… please," I begged, unable to stop.

He pushed it in a little ways. My whole body arched up off the table, in anticipation of his thrust.

"Are you my little whore?" Carl asked in a quiet voice that made me look up into his face, my eyes going very wide. The idea that he could ask the filthy question so sweetly seemed to overwhelm my mind. When I saw the smile on his lips, the affection and the wolfish need, I felt my heart would burst.

"Yes, master," I whispered, as I felt him put his hands around my narrow waist just under the stiff fabric of the bustier, gripping me there, seeming to ready me for his utter possession of my body. "I'm your little whore. Please… please fuck me."

 *sabella*

Carl thrust his cock into me so hard then, so deep into me, all the way until I seemed to feel his rigid penis press against my ribs. His hands tightened around my waist, and I felt so mastered, so controlled and yet so safe and loved that it literally seemed like I had entered a dream.

I looked up into his dark eyes, saw him studying me as if he meant to possess me with his gaze, his mind even, as well as with his hardness.

"You may come," he said. His voice sounded hard—not quite as low as the voice of authority, maybe, but very commanding. His eyes, though, as he gave me that permission I needed so very badly, had a softness to them, and his lips a little smile. I could tell that he had spoken so dominantly out of sheer masculine instinct, and I loved him for having that instinct because as soon as I saw the kindness in his eyes I started to come, harder than I had ever imagined I could.

My body seemed to go white hot with the pleasure. Every muscle tensed, fighting Carl's grip as he started to fuck me in a hard, quick rhythm. His lap pounded into my bottom over and over. I held on to the backs of my knees, pulling and spreading even more, suddenly desperate to show my sponsor how well the body he had given me could take his cock and give it the pleasure he deserved.

"Oh..." Carl grunted, and I couldn't help smiling myself through the reason-destroying ecstasy of those chained orgasms that kept on jolting through me. I saw in his face that the sensation inside me had taken him by surprise, that his nervous system had filled with a pleasure greater than he had expected... maybe more than he had ever felt, just as my own body seemed to whisper, *Oh, so this is what it's supposed to feel like.*

I cried out just at the thought, and my body tensed against Carl's hands and my own hands. The tension, the little bit of resistance to the dominance my sponsor, my owner, had imposed on my new, sexy shape, sent me into another climax, this one so titanic that I knew that after it I would merely lie limp under my master's thrusting manhood.

That following idea, the picture of my unresisting body, my too-full pussy, just taking the rigid penis as long and as hard as Carl wanted to give it to me, brought a sob from my chest. At the same time, just as I felt my muscles relax, he pulled his cock out of my pussy.

I looked up, my lips parting in surprise, and then I gasped as I understood what my new master meant to do. His eyes had moved down my body, and my face blazed with heat because I knew what that gaze had fixed on.

"Oh…" I whispered. "Oh… please… no… not yet?"

His fingertips probed inside my pussy and my back arched as I cried out at an aftershock of my huge orgasm. I felt him gathering the wetness inside me, and he looked up again, into my eyes, studying my pouting, needy face.

"I'll be gentle, Isabella," he promised, his face concerned but resolute. "I need to take you anally, though. Right now."

I felt my eyes widen at the word *need*. A surge of heat came to my cheeks—and down below to the pussy where his fingers were still discovering my arousal. The sudden, mortifying need *I* felt for that terribly degrading, filthy act… the need to *be* taken that way—to serve my owner with my tightest, most private hole made me close my eyes in shame.

"Need," I whispered.

I felt his fingers withdraw from my vagina and move down. I felt, on the tiny entrance, just how much lubrication he had found in my pussy to help him take my ass.

My heart-shaped ass… my gorgeous rear-end… the kind a husband should be proud to own… to claim… to take his pleasure inside no matter how obscene and dirty bottom-fucking might seem.

219

I cried out at the entry of his finger, the way he prepared me for the cock. I opened my eyes again to find Carl's attention down there. His gaze flicked up to mine and narrowed... stayed on my face as he expertly added a second finger to the first. I whimpered, my backside squirming in mingled discomfort and pleasure, the discomfort somehow adding to the pleasure.

"I'll punish you this way too, my dear," he murmured, "when you're very naughty."

The two fingers pressed more firmly, as if to demonstrate exactly what Carl meant. I mewed like a kitten desperate for milk, hearing in the noise just how effectively my sponsor could discipline me this way if he chose.

I had thought only a few moments before that the erotic response inside my pussy, in my tingling clit, had reached its limit. The faint pleasure I felt now in Carl's lewd invasion of my virginal bottom, my panties pulled aside, first for ordinary fucking, and then for this darker kind of possession, reawakened my need terribly and seemed to focus it through the alarm, the fluttery nervousness in my tummy.

The idea that my sponsor would not take no for an answer where my new ass was concerned, that he needed to fuck me in that unnatural way and so he would, whether I wanted him there or not... I moaned as he returned his attention to preparing me to receive him in the place whose tightness would give him pleasure at the expense of my pain.

I looked down between my legs to see him pumping his hard cock in his left hand while he trained my bottom with his right. I couldn't see the fingers that moved steadily inside my anus, only the heel of his hand, but that motion made me feel faint with the humiliating knowledge of the use to which Carl would soon put my bottom.

He took that hand away. I felt my forehead crease with shame and need as I watched him watch his own hard penis press against my smallest hole. I tightened with a little whimper, and Carl's eyes rose to meet mine as he kept pushing gently with the somehow both firm and soft head of his massive cock.

"Shh, Isabella. Let me in. You know how."

"Oh God," I whispered. "It... master... it hurts."

"I know," Carl replied. "I'll be gentle. Just let me in and you'll start to get used to it. An ass like this one deserves fucking, though. You're going to have a lot of it."

My head swiveled side to side, hair threshing back and forth as I kept looking at my sponsor's face despite the movement, trying to figure out why I wanted, despite the discomfort, to give him this forbidden pleasure at the expense of my own.

You're going to have... deserves fucking... with a whimpering cry I pushed, and I opened, fire blazing in my cheeks as I felt it happen.

A sound of satisfaction came from deep in Carl's chest, a rumbling *mmm* that to my surprise turned some of the sensation coming from my anus into pleasure... into a clench of my pussy. I clutched the backs of my knees more tightly, feeling the fishnet mesh sliding under my fingers. My hips bucked, offering my pussy desperately to my master.

The rumbling sound of his pleasure continued. He had looked down again, a smile coming to his lips as if in simple enjoyment of the sight of himself possessing me so degradingly, laid out in my sexy lingerie on the lunch table, my panties pulled aside for his shameful pleasure.

"Yes, good girl," he murmured, the words in place of the growl just as deep and just as rumbly, so that my forlorn, empty vagina clenched again. "You need it bad, don't you. Would you like to come with my cock in your magnificent ass?"

"Oh God... Carl..."

His eyes rose, widening slightly, his smile broadening. As I heard his first name pass my lips for the very first time, I had a moment of tingling fear that he might be angry I had called him by it, with such familiarity. It made me gasp, because again, at the thought he might punish me, my pussy had clenched.

And though his smile remained warm, he took advantage of the opportunity. Even as his knowing fingers found my clit and began to caress it with impossible, paradoxical gentleness, he said, "We'll have a little discipline session for that later, Isabella," and at the same time he leaned forward to drive his hardness deep into my anus.

"Oh God... Carl..." I felt my face go crimson as I realized I had done it again. "Mr. Thring," I added, "oh, please." For a moment, oddly, I felt like I might cry, thinking that because I hadn't addressed him properly my sponsor wouldn't let me have the orgasm he had offered.

The special orgasm... the idea of it, to come with the cock in my bottom, while he rode me in my most forbidden place, used me in the most degrading way I could imagine... maybe not the biggest orgasm, but...

I cried out, because Carl had started rubbing my clit again as he began to fuck my bottom.

I did come, looking into my master's eyes while he possessed me, his rhythm slow and steady. With a moan I felt my bottom much too full of cock, and the filthy sensation seemed to send little rockets of submissive pleasure traveling from my wide-stretched anus to the tender, tingling nub his fingers fondled, tracing little circles around the sensitive spot.

The tiny orgasms made me tighten on his rigid manhood and the extra discomfort and fullness made me cry out piteously. I saw the hunger it brought to Carl's face, and he really did look for a moment like a wolf. The thought made me clench again, cry out again, and then, with a cry of his own, Carl held himself inside my bottom very deep, his lap jerking against my bottom. I felt his cock pulse and another surge of heat rushed to my cheeks at the sheer lewdness of the sensation.

"Oh God," I sobbed. "Master... oh..."

He bent down and kissed me, his weight mostly on his arms but enough of it coming on top of me that I could vividly feel my new body, my huge breasts, pressed down by my sponsor's form, his muscular limbs, his massive upper body. I let out another sob into his mouth, clutching my knees hard, wishing I could hold him.

Carl must have sensed it, for he said in the voice, "Put your arms around me."

His hard, massive penis had started to grow softer in my bottom, but it still felt too big there, my ass too full of cock. As I obeyed him, clinging to him with a whimper from deep in my throat, I took a strange refuge in that feeling—my sponsor had decided I should still have his manhood in my smallest hole—he meant me to remember how thoroughly he had claimed me.

He picked me up off the table. I gasped and clung to him even harder, not understanding. Carl began to carry me then, with his penis in my anus, toward the door of the dining room.

"What?" I giggled into his ear, suddenly overcome by the absurdity. "You... Carl, you can't."

I heard the smile in his reply. "So you know, you may call me Carl when my cock is soft. When I punish you in a little while it will be for addressing me that way when we were having sex. And yes, I can."

He did. As I thought about what he had just said, trying to figure out whether he was joking and deciding that, no, his rule actually made sense to me, my sponsor carried me to my bedroom with his cock in my ass, through my bedroom to the sumptuous bathroom.

When we had reached the bidet, he lifted me off his penis at last and set me on my feet. He kept holding me in his arms, though, and I kept clinging to him, until at last he spoke again.

"I want to watch you wash up," he said simply. "Go ahead and use the bidet for me."

CHAPTER 25

 arl

Her bathroom session that morning had made it clear how powerful a role the bidet played in Isabella's erotic imagination. I didn't need Selecta's help—though of course they had provided it in the form of a summarizing email—to know that I would have a lot of fun in the bathroom with my new bed girl, my stunning girlfriend, my prospective bride.

And if I had maintained the slightest doubt that my own erotic predilection for dominating a girl in the bathroom had a counterpart in Isabella's newly awakened submission, the look in her eyes when I told her to clean her pussy and anus would have confirmed it. Her eyes went wide and her face went red.

"But…" she said, the look of dismay on her face so arousing that despite the quiescent, well-satisfied state of my cock I felt a little leap down there.

"But what?" I asked, raising one eyebrow. I spoke playfully, but I also added an edge to my tone to suggest the possibility of consequences, and in particular the sort of consequences that always have a special allure when administered in the very special space of a splendidly outfitted bathroom.

Isabella's brow furrowed, and she sucked her lower lip into her mouth. Her eyes pleaded with me, but she had no further words of protest.

"But that's private?" I asked, arching my eyebrow still further. "My dear, I promise I'll give you privacy when you need it, but I'll also be in control of your body whenever I choose. I'm going to watch you wash up, and then I'm going to punish you for calling me by my first name when I had my cock inside you."

The crease on her forehead grew deeper. A flash of doubt suddenly flickered across her features, as if she had wondered suddenly whether I truly meant it the way it would certainly have sounded to some clinical outside observer.

Well, probably not the clinical outside observers who actually *were* listening, the ones from Selecta, who would dutifully record that I had expressed my dominance over my Selecta girl in a constructive fashion. Someone *not* employed by the megacorp who had transformed Isabella's body into the stunning shape of her dreams and delivered that body to me might well have misperceived that expression as an intolerably chauvinistic, even criminal way to speak to the girl I loved.

"Don't make it worse, Isabella," I said quietly and intently. All my dominant instincts told me to give her time to work it out in her head—my real intent and her real need for what I meant to give her. "I'm going to plug your bottom as a punishment and spank you in the tub. That spanking could be much longer, though, if you decide not to obey me."

Isabella's lips had parted, and her incredible breasts, still encased in the gorgeous, stiffened silk of the bustier, heaved up and down with her labored breathing.

"You're..." she whispered. She swallowed very hard. "You're... sir... Mr. Thring... You're..."

I waited patiently, looking into her eyes. I felt the slight smile on my lips widen a bit.

Isabella bit her lip, and her nostrils flared as the heavy breathing got redirected through her adorable nose.

"You're... playing?" she tried, as if she hadn't quite figured out how to say what she really meant.

I smiled even more broadly. I knew from long consideration and experience that in fact she had hit on the best—maybe the only good—way to talk about it.

"Depends on what you mean," I said, though, slowly and gently. "But yes. I'm definitely playing. I'm playing with my new toy. My new plaything."

* * *

Isabella

I gasped.

I could see in Carl's eyes that he knew exactly what I had meant. I had meant to ask if he was serious—if he really intended to discipline me like a naughty child or a disobedient pet, but by means much more degrading and shameful than anyone, any guardian or sponsor or master, would ever really use.

No matter how firm-handed a man might think himself, no matter how much wealth he might have... he—Carl—couldn't be serious, could he? Because I had spoken his *first name* at the wrong moment?

But his response... *his new toy.* I felt my face working, tears forming at the corners of my eyes. Distress, yes, but of a kind that seemed to make me pant with need despite myself and despite the wrenching climaxes Carl had brought to my new body such a short time ago. Despite even the way he had used my anus and how strange and open I felt back there now.

He couldn't... he couldn't put a plug in there, could he? Everyone knew about butt plugs; funny pictures of them littered the Selecta Arrangements forums. I had always thought that only, well, weird kinky people actually... *used* them. And I had honestly supposed that when girls on the forums mentioned *discipline* with butt plugs, they were 100% joking.

Even so, I had always navigated away from those posts immediately, ignoring the ambiguity of the chill that had gone down my spine at the hint of a connection between a young woman's anus and the need some SA members felt to take her in hand. I felt that chill as I looked into Carl's serious and yet also somehow playful eyes, and I understood that it was, in fact, not a chill but a *thrill*—a thrill of desperate, wanton need.

"But..." I whispered, my mind searching for the words, any words that might capture the thing I so needed to know.

His smile had nearly vanished for a moment as he contemplated me, and the hunger had seemed to reawaken in his eyes. I knew with a surge of heat that my distress turned him on, made him hard. I wanted to look down and see whether his cock—*his amazing cock*, my brain added, strangely and giddily, to my astonishment—had grown again. That urge made my eyes go wide, and I saw Carl smile again as if he could guess precisely how it aroused me to have him master me this way.

I took a sharp breath. I had it. "But you won't do it unless you're sure I need it. You won't play with your toy unless it's good... unless it's right for me." I felt a tear well up and run down my cheek—not even of distress, but of wild joy.

His smile got even wider, and his arms closed around me even more tightly. He bent down and kissed me gently, and then more urgently, so that I whimpered up into his mouth. Then he let go and stepped away. The look in his eyes had gotten fierce and his smile had gone. "Do as I've told you, Isabella. Wash your cunt and your bottom. Then I'll plug you, and we'll take a bath."

I closed my eyes and let out a deep, sobbing breath. For a long moment I seemed to stay suspended there, and my mind's eye traveled out of my body. I had started to get very used to that detached, floating feeling, and even to welcome it for its calmness and the way it seemed to change shame and pain to pleasure. The idea of a bath in the enormous, gorgeous jacuzzi tub seemed so out of keeping with the idea of discipline that it brought confusion and alarm and thrilling anticipation to my mind and my body almost in equal measure.

I could see myself behind my closed lids, standing in front of the bidet with my panties askew from the thorough fucking my sponsor had given me, the fishnets and bustier still encasing my legs and my ribs and my amazing breasts. The white lingerie, now completely belied by the use to which Carl had already put me... by the trickle of his seed I could feel coming from my newly-open anus.

I gave a full sob, and I started to back up, bending my knees, with my eyes still closed. My feet shuffled apart. I heard something clicking and a metallic creak to my right. Halfway into a crouch over the bidet, I saw that Carl had opened the medicine cabinet behind the mirror and taken out...

Oh, it's too big, my mind cried out. *It's much too big.*

Pink, to match the bathroom. Four or five inches long and at least two inches thick at its widest spot. The bulbous curves and the flared plug, to make sure it wouldn't go all the way up inside me but would instead stay exactly where my owner wanted to put it, opening my bottom to punish me for my misbehavior and to remind me of how he liked to fuck me there.

I turned my head to look up at Carl as he brandished the pink toy casually in front of me. He smiled slightly, but his eyes remained narrow, as if he wanted to drink in and to assess every tiny detail of my reaction to his humiliating discipline.

Playing. He's playing... with me. Playing me. Oh God.

I bit my lip. I needed something more, I suddenly realized, having seen the terrible thing he meant to put in my anus.

Carl gave it to me. He spoke in the voice.

"Go ahead, Isabella," he said quietly but with the utmost authority. "Do as I told you. Why don't you take your panties off, first of all."

I gave a little cry as my body obeyed him much more eagerly than I wanted it to. I hooked my thumbs into the narrow waistband and I pulled down the thong, frowning with the embarrassment of having to do that intensely private thing in front of him. With my eyes on the tiled floor, I spread my feet further apart and I crouched over the bidet.

"Look at me," Carl said, still using the voice. A whimper came from my throat just as I raised my eyes, because the warm water had started at that moment too, and the soothing flow of it against my pussy and my bottom reawakened the intensity of feeling I had known on the table in the dining room with my master's hardness inside me.

He moved to my left side, and he stooped and he reached the terrifying pink plug down under me, between my legs.

"Put soap on it, my dear," he said in his normal voice, "while you're washing yourself. To make it go in easier."

Automatically, I reached my own hands down to take the thing. My breath caught in my throat as I touched its firm but slightly yielding silicone surface. Carl had let go of it and turned it over to me, as if to let me get acquainted with the implement of my punishment. He stood up, and my eyes went wide as he began rapidly to strip off all his clothes.

"Oh…" I whispered at the sight of his taut upper body, his hairy chest. He smiled, clearly knowing just how good he looked naked. My eyes went to his cock, semi-hard again already and getting visibly harder. Between my thighs, my right hand couldn't help a little naughtiness with the warm water. Two fingers found the place my sponsor had put that huge penis and reminded me of how it had satisfied the ache there, at least for a little while.

His clothes off and laid aside, he returned to me.

"Are you playing with yourself, my dear?" he asked, though in a playful rather than a severe way—not as if it would worsen my punishment.

"I can't help it," I whispered, feeling a theatrically wanton pout come onto my face and enjoying the knowledge of how it would make my owner's cock even more rigid, more ready for me.

My hand had found the soap even as I looked only at Carl. I used it as much to increase the pleasure down there as to obey his orders and wash my pussy and bottom. I heard my breathing grow increasingly labored against the plash of the water in the bidet.

"Well, you'd better clean my cock too," he said, and then he moved back in front of me and presented his manhood, throbbing and lengthening even as I watched.

For a moment a dark, filthy image came into my mind, and my hips jerked at the forbidden thought. I reached up, though, with my soapy hands, and cleaned my master in the conventional way first… and then, when I had soaped the rigid length and rinsed it thoroughly, I did the dirty thing and tasted the clean cock while I played with my pussy and even put my own soapy finger in my own well-fucked asshole.

CHAPTER 26

sabella

Carl stroked my hair and murmured, "Good girl." A warmth spread from the water between my legs all the way through my body. His pleasure seemed somehow wired to mine, as if the new body Selecta had given me at his behest were simply that attuned to my sponsor's enjoyment.

Gently he pulled his penis from between my lips. I looked up at him, a tentative smile on my lips, the plug and its discipline forgotten as it lay in the bidet. I just... I just *loved* him. I remembered the plug, and I blushed, and I still loved him—I loved him even more for knowing what I needed and giving it to me.

"Let's get you out of these things," Carl murmured, and then he started to undress me while I luxuriated—that's

235

what it felt like—on the bidet. Not just a dirty little French whore, but a *pampered*, dirty little French whore. "You keep playing with that little cunt."

"Oh my God," I whispered as he removed the high-heeled pump from my right foot, lifting it off the tile gently and freeing my toes. I liked sexy shoes but taking them off always gave me a sweet feeling of release. That feeling had never, ever felt so sweet before, as the man who had bought me (how could I avoid that thought?) and used me acted like a servant, while I frankly and lewdly played with myself.

I let out a little whimpering moan as he rolled down the stocking on that leg and tugged it off, again gently raising my foot. My forehead creased and I closed my eyes, my fingers still helplessly busy with my soapy clit—not building toward an orgasm but just... luxuriating. Just enjoying this moment of service from the man I had decided I had no choice but to serve, even if I could have come up with a single reason not to yield myself up to him, body and soul.

I heard him step around me to the other side of the bidet. He took off my left shoe, rolled down my left stocking. I made little whimpering noises in my throat and felt them emerge through my lips, the lower one held firmly in my teeth. The submissive sound brought a surge of heat to my cheeks but also down below, and I realized with a start that made me open my eyes that I could actually feel myself enjoying my shame.

At that moment, Carl started to unzip the bustier, and I let out a little cry of surprise at the sudden feeling of nakedness—real nakedness in front of my sponsor for the first time in my fully developed new body. Freed from the support of the bustier's cups, my enormous breasts hung heavily on my chest, and to my amazement I realized that for the rest of my life—or, I supposed, until Selecta gave me the pill that would change me back—I would have a very different relationship with bras than I had ever had before. I had always thought them a necessary accoutrement for a polished appearance. Now I knew them to be a necessity for comfort.

That rational thought, though, went away completely when Carl dropped the bustier to the side and from behind took hold of those heavy peaches—*no... gourds... melons, even,* I thought with a blush—in his hands. The wide grip of his long fingers and his broad palms could just barely hold all of my breasts, my nipples between his middle fingers. He pinched a little with those fingers as he weighed the melons in his grasp, and a sob came from my throat at the feeling of dominance, the simple arrogance of having him just take hold of my breasts that way, as if he had that right whenever he chose.

Between my thighs my fingers suddenly became more urgent, and my hips bounced with the clench that had just thrilled through my pussy.

"So nice," Carl murmured in my ear. "You are so fucking gorgeous, Isabella."

My lips parted and my breath grew ragged as what had seemed a moment before a simple soothing touch between my thighs grew into a compulsion.

"You may keep masturbating," he told me, "while I put in your plug."

"Oh no," I whispered, but to my astonishment my body responded despite Carl's not even having used a hint of the voice. I raised myself on my knees, and I arched my back to push out my backside... my big heart-shaped bottom. I felt the spreading of the cheeks and it made my fingers even busier between my thighs at the hot flash of shame that sensation brought, the terrible immodesty of showing my tiny anus to my master.

Not so tiny anymore, I thought with a little gasp of need and pleasure. Below me, in the basin of the bidet, I watched Carl's right hand take the plug, and then I heard the faint, slippery sound of him soaping it.

It touched me... it touched the most private place on my body...

Not so private, anymore, either. The thought sent an electric jolt of pleasure from my clit into my hips. I cried out at its strength, and it gained even more at the way it made my bottom push even further backward, as if to impale my anus on the plug. At the same time, though, it tightened the sensitive ring of muscle so that instead of welcoming my punishment the way an obedient bed girl should, I pushed the toy away.

Carl's left hand gripped my waist to steady me and keep me in place. My hand responded, two fingers going deep into my pussy, trying to satisfy the aching need for his hardness that suddenly arose there. I found the g-spot, pressed it, cried out.

"Don't come," my sponsor said in the voice of authority. "Open this bottom for me."

"Oh no…" I breathed. "Oh, please…"

But my body had already responded. I pulled my hand away from my pussy and I pushed on the inside, with the shameful skill I had learned on the table in the dining room. Then I gave a little scream of alarm and discomfort as Carl pushed an inch of the plug inside me.

"Are you going to address me properly?" he growled.

"Oh my God," I moaned. "Oh my God… oh my God."

He kept pushing. I sobbed with discomfort.

He eased the pressure, pulled the plug out a little, leaving the tip inside, though now my tiny ring tried to expel it.

"Are you, my dear?" Carl said and he began to push again.

"No… please… I mean…" It kept pushing, and with a whimpering cry I pushed too, in the right way, to open myself shamefully, and the soapy plug went inside me. "Yes… oh God… sir, please…"

"Good girl," my sponsor said as I let out a sobbing sigh of relief at the sensation of my anus closing, at least a little, around the narrow base of the plug. Now the terrible fullness of my bottom became the dominant sensation in my body, my world.

I put my right hand back between my thighs, felt the silicone base of the toy nestled lewdly between the roundness of my newly shapely cheeks. With a cry of alarm and helpless need I moved my fingers forward and found my clit in its wrinkly folds, a burning nub of arousal. I rubbed myself there frantically, trying to make it feel better, trying to ease the fullness a little.

And Carl didn't delay in making that feeling even more intense. As if overcome by the sexiness of the wanton, shameful view he had of my punished bottom and my naughty fingers, he used his left hand to raise my backside a little further off the bidet and he moved forward far enough to put the head of his cock at the entrance to my aching sheath.

"Oh, please..." I whispered. I left off the *no* that I had thought I would add—had to add—because at that moment Carl started, slowly and gently, to enter me, and fill me much, much too full of his firm-handed discipline, his possessive pleasure.

"You may come," he murmured into my ear as he crouched over me, his mouth so close I could feel the breath of his words. He kissed my neck and held me by the haunches and started to fuck me over the bidet.

I came... and came... and came. Carl fucked me softly, so that I could feel every inch of his cock as he moved it in and out of my needy but increasingly sore pussy. The pain itself made me come, and I shuddered in his grasp. He kept kissing me—my chin, my cheek, my ear—but he stilled his hardness' movement after my third orgasm.

I moaned to feel him so deep, with the plug in my bottom making me feel like my master had utterly appropriated my new body for his pleasure.

"We're going to go to the tub now," he said in a low voice.

I realized that the sound of running water had filled the air of the bathroom for the last few minutes. Maybe Carl had turned it on with some kind of remote control, or maybe the Selecta researchers had done it. I blushed at that thought, remembering that they had watched all the shameful things that had just happened over the bidet.

Carl pulled his rigid penis slowly out of me, and then he stood me up and took me by the hand and led me to the enormous tub, where the steam rose enticingly and the jacuzzi jets had already started to roil the water. I hobbled and shuffled, biting my lip over the little whimpers that emerged with every step, at the feeling of having the punishment plug deep in my backside.

I turned to him, and looked up into his face, doing my best to ignore the splendid, hairy, completely naked rest of his muscular body. "You're going to... to..." My heart felt fluttery, though I didn't really know why, since I had already endured so much.

"I'm going to spank you in the tub, Isabella," he said, nodding slowly.

Spank. Was it just the word? Yes, partly... but... also the idea of my older sponsor, my wealthy, powerful owner, administering discipline and care in what seemed like equal measure. I felt ambiguous tears—shame and happiness somehow mingled together—well up in my eyes. My next words seemed destined, like a young woman in this position, a bed girl, simply had to say them.

"Do you have to?" I asked. "Sir?"

The corners of Carl's mouth turned up. "Yes, my dear," he said very gently. "I have to."

I felt my face crumple as I nodded, and the tears fell onto my cheeks, but inside my heart thrilled at his firmness.

"Step into the tub," he told me, using the voice of authority. "Kneel on the seat over there and push out your bottom for me to show you're grateful for my discipline."

He still had hold of my hand, and he helped me into the wonderful warm water. I couldn't even have said why I felt scared of the spanking, since I knew so much about my body and my needs, and I knew so much about Carl. The idea of this kind of spanking, so clearly intended as an act of love as much as of discipline, still carried a delicious current of shame, though. The idea of a thirty-year-old given a sexy body for her owner's pleasure and then spanked like a little girl... the picture of myself in my mind's eye, getting ready for a spanking in the bathtub... *oh God...*

It was my wanton need that scared me, I realized. The boundless, yawning desire for a firm-handed master who would use me as he liked. I trembled despite the soothing warmth of the water, reaching up my thighs as I knelt on the seat, almost reaching to my full bottom, the magnificent ass Carl had given me, with Selecta's help.

"Put your head down," my sponsor said, and I did, gratefully resting my face on my outstretched arms, which I reached over the side of the tub, where Selecta had put cushions as if for just such a discipline session.

Carl stood outside the huge tub, to my side. He put his left hand on my shoulder, steadying me, and with his right he started to spank my bare bottom with sharp slaps that echoed off the tile.

He spanked me slowly this time, alternating from side to side. I let out a little whimpering, kittenish sound with each spank, but to my surprise they didn't really hurt. Each slap made my ass feel warmer and fuller, until I sobbed not from pain but from the excess of sensation. I had completely lost track of how long Carl had been disciplining me that way, my consciousness floating off toward the tiled ceiling, when he stopped, and I heard and felt him getting into the tub behind me.

I knew what was coming, and I cried out as I felt him starting to pull the plug from my bottom. I pushed and moaned, and at last it came out. I knew—something about the way he had spanked me, or rubbed my shoulder, seemed to have let me read his darkest needs—and so I arched my back and raised my ass, so he could take me again along that forbidden path.

EMILY TILTON

I cried out again, feeling him fill me with cock, holding my anus open with his thrusting hardness. My master seemed to feel no need to be gentle this time. With his hand between my thighs to hold my pussy possessively while he fucked my bottom, he rode hard, and I cried out to learn his rough ways.

"Oh, Isabella... so... good," he grunted as he used me. I felt his climax build, and I knew my new body pleased him— and not just my new body, but the transformation, and even the very idea of the transformation. I had submitted myself to it, to become his new plaything. His cock grew so rigid I thought he would stretch my tiny ring too far, but instead he held himself in deep and came inside me again, his bearded lips against my throat, kissing me gently even as he enjoyed me so brutally with his manhood.

"Thank you," he murmured into my ear. "Such a good girl. Such a marvelous toy."

The End

AFTERWORD

Stormy Night Publications would like to thank you for your interest in our books.

If you liked this book (or even if you didn't), we would really appreciate you leaving a review on the site where you purchased it. Reviews provide useful feedback for us and our authors, and this feedback (both positive comments and constructive criticism) allows us to work even harder to make sure we provide the content our customers want to read.

If you would like to check out more books from Stormy Night Publications, if you want to learn more about our company, or if you would like to join our mailing list, please visit our website at:

http://www.stormynightpublications.com

THE INSTITUTE: SHAMEFUL ARRANGEMENTS SERIES

Her Shameful Arrangement

Her Billionaire's Demands

THE INSTITUTE SERIES

THE INSTITUTE: NAUGHTY LITTLE GIRLS SERIES

The Oak Street Method: Wendy

The Oak Street Method: Ginnie

The Oak Street Method: Frankie and Mary

The Oak Street Method: Heather

The Oak Street Method: Renee

Beyond Oak Street: Their Billionaire Daddies

THE INSTITUTE: BAD GIRLS SERIES

BOUND FOR SERVICE SERIES

BEYOND THE INSTITUTE: THE FUTURE OF CORRECTION SERIES

CORPORATE CORRECTION SERIES

SHAMEFULLY COURTED SERIES

His Blushing Bride

Claimed as His Bride

Her Shameful Lesson

Her Shameful Wedding Night

The Doctor's Girl

VICTORIAN CORRECTION SERIES

GALACTIC DISCIPLINE SERIES

MORE STORMY NIGHT BOOKS BY EMILY TILTON

EMILY TILTON LINKS

You can keep up with Emily Tilton via her newsletter, her Facebook page, and her Goodreads profile, using the following links:

https://landing.mailerlite.com/webforms/ landing/k8d6a9

https://www.facebook.com/pages/Explorations-by-Emily-Tilton/524106554315976

http://www.goodreads.com/author/show/ 7048431.Emily_Tilton

Made in the USA
Middletown, DE
01 October 2022

11659896R00156